The Adventures of Caterwaul the Cat

Feline Pie

By
Damon Plumides & Arthur Mark Boerke

The Adventures of Caterwaul the Cat: Feline Pie
© 2010 Damon Plumides and Arthur Mark Boerke. All Rights Reserved.
www.caterwaulthecat.com

First edition.

This is a work of fiction. All of the characters, names, incidents, organizations, and dialogue in this novel are either the products of the authors' imaginations or are used fictitiously.

Published in the U.S. by BQB Publishing Company
www.bqbpublishing.com

Printed in the United States of America

ISBN 978-1-937084-19-6 (p)
ISBN 978-1-937084-20-2 (e)

Library of Congress Control Number: 2011940285

Book cover and interior illustrations by Daniel Edwards
Book interior by Robin Krauss, Linden Design, www.lindendesign.biz

Dedication

This book is dedicated with love to the memory of Ann M. Boerke, Michael George Plumides Sr., and Diana Boerke. We miss you all. We'd also like to dedicate our work to Arthur's recently passed mentor, Dr. Owen "Mike" Connelly, who stoked a fire in Arthur to create and become both a professor and a writer. Last but not least, as they say, this book is also dedicated to the newest addition to our Caterwaul family, Michael Damon Plumides, a.k.a. Wiggles Paisan.

~ Arthur & Damon ~

Acknowledgments

Working on this book was a labor of love for the both of us. It was a true collaboration that neither one of us would have been able to produce without the other. For some parts, Damon would come up with the basic plot and characters, and Arthur would flesh out the story and the dialogue; in other parts, Arthur would cut loose with a run of storyline, and Damon would swoop in to help polish it off and tweak some of the humor. When all was said and done, however, the end result proved to be a story woven with heart and soul—ours—and of which we are extremely proud.

Some of the wonderful people who either helped us directly in bringing this work to light or by inspiring us creatively include Daphne Aycock and John Fuller, without whom we might still be dreaming of finding an outlet for our creative expression; our publisher, Terri Leidich of Boutique of Quality Books, whom Arthur met at a book convention in Columbia, South Carolina; as well as Lisa Schindler, our daily contact with the publishing company, who helped keep us on track and connected us with other creative people. Our thanks also go out to Lori K. Lee and Jeff Plucker of BQB, who are parts of the great team dedicated to bringing this book and all BQB authors' works to the general public.

A very special thank you goes out to our editor, Martin Coffee, who helped us polish off this manuscript while leaving our voice and vision untouched. Martin, we will work with you anytime! Special thanks go out to Dan Edwards, our cover and interior illustrator, for doing such a fine job on the artwork. We would also like to extend our gratitude to Patrick, Psychonaut13, Coffield for designing our web page for us.

Our great appreciation goes out to our friends and family, who were so supportive from the beginning. These include in no particular order: Roger Skaw; Derek Chiarenza; Michael George Plumides Jr.; Rhiannon Hendren; Anne Saunders; Kat Taylor; Lauren and Sophia; George Plumides; Ali Plumides; Justin Kates our photographer; Jack Boerke; Scott Moore for some inspired interpretations of our hero Caterwaul; Robert "Robbie" Lewis for his constant encouragement; Fred Bisogno Sr. for the Italian lesson; Fred Bisogno Jr. for more than thirty years of friendship; Donna and Ken Reese; Anastasia Hendren; Robin Penley Jones; Brett Jones; Robin Sharpe; Jeremy Hendren; Kim Gallant Revels; Katherine Gallant; Tonya Douglass Beth Stevenson; Louanne Smith; Stacey Steifel; Kevin "Mickey" Boerke; Tracey Waters; Tonya Kelly; and Megan and Ben Magri and the Magri Family for their support very early on.

The authors also want to acknowledge anyone who read part or all of the manuscript in its evolving form, who offered suggestions or support in any way, and anyone who has watched this project grow from an idea into the novel that is in your hands now. There is no way that we could possibly list you all and, for that, we apologize. Just know that the authors appreciate all the support you have given us along the way, and we hope that you enjoy the story.

The Tale of the Tail

J first met Damon Plumides many years ago when he was the singer in the Myrtle Beach-based, hard rock band called Dead Cut Tree. At the time, I was an owner and talent buyer for the legendary Columbia, South Carolina, nightclub Rockafellas'. I used to book Dead Cut Tree to play shows at Rockafellas' on a regular basis. Over time, we became the best of friends.

Years later, we would share a house together in Charlotte. I was now a university history professor, while Damon worked as a wine consultant. Both of us still had our creative juices inside us, but needed something to get them flowing again. Then one day Damon came to me with a few pages hand-scrawled in pen on yellow legal paper. Busy with grading or some such chore, I at first wanted to shove the pages in a pile. Boy, am I glad I didn't, because what he had written on those several pages was a rough outline of a fantastic children's story. He wanted me to help him to turn it into something much more. This was the beginning of the collaboration that would give rise to *The Adventures of Caterwaul the Cat: Feline Pie.*

This novel is in every way a dual effort with the characters, jokes, and plot scenarios created by both of us. The sum reward of our creative partnership on this book would never have been possible for one of us without the participation of the other. We sincerely hope that you enjoy reading about our world as much as we enjoyed creating it for you.

~ Arthur Mark "Art" Boerke ~

Table of "Cat"tents

Prologue

The black cat tiptoed silently as he slid past the green glowing globe. His furry body hugged the cave wall as he moved. It appeared as though the sheen of his coat absorbed the pale light as he went, preventing the casting of his shadow in the dimness.

Caterwaul planned his escape more than a year ago, moving slowly and methodically to avoid suspicion, learning about anything and everything he might need on the outside.

Funny that he chose the expression "on the outside." He thought about it a moment and allowed himself a sort of half-smile. After all, he hardly remembered what his life was like as a kitten, before she'd gotten hold of him, so he really couldn't know what to expect.

Peering back over his shoulder, he saw the old woman who had been his companion these last few years. She was frail and ancient looking. She sat, as she often did, asleep in her favorite rickety chair. Her head slumped back against the broken mesh of woven grass, mouth open to reveal a collection of yellowed and missing teeth. He was sure she was asleep because her left eye was open and completely motionless. A cloudy white film worked to obscure the eye's natural brown pigment. Occasionally, a high-pitched snore would escape her open maw, and every so often, she'd make a gurgling sound before resuming her routine.

Over time Caterwaul learned quite a bit about conjuring from watching the old woman work. A lot of it was what might be put down as simple garden-variety stuff, but there were some spells among his gleanings that could only be called sorcery.

He had filled a pack with whatever he imagined he might need: spells he'd written down, potions and powders, roots and reagents, tokens, and talismans. Once free, he had no plan of ever returning to that cave.

Arriving at the entrance, he noticed that the door had been left slightly ajar. The cat squeezed his frame through the narrow space between the door and its jamb and sprinted up the earthen ramp in the direction of daylight. What luck it was that the rat left it cracked as he had. His heart began to race, and he unconsciously increased his speed as he approached the cave opening.

He caught the eyes of several small cave creatures, but they were too involved with their own business to cause him any trouble. The one potential problem was the rat. The rat was unpredictable.

Caterwaul prayed the filthy bugger was off in a ditch somewhere, intoxicated, sleeping off the effects of some over-fermented hunk of fruit he'd been saving for a special occasion.

Luckily there was no sign of the rodent, or any other resistance, as he emerged into the cool of the early evening's breeze. "So far so good," he whispered.

Now outside, his best course of action was to follow a shallow creek leading away from the cave. As he crept along the stream, a small turtle popped his head from the water and sneezed. This startled the cat, and he slipped, his forepaws ending up in the muddy water.

"Sorry about that chief," the small turtle said apologetically. "I know your kind doesn't usually care for water." He swam toward the creek's edge and sat down on a slab of water-polished slate. He had a face that was painted with yellow and black stripes and a lacquered orange underbelly quite intricate in design.

"So you're headed up along the creek, eh?" he asked Caterwaul. "Not sure if that's such a good idea at the moment." The turtle put a claw to his lips as to signal for silence. "Something, or someone, has those frogs up in arms again."

"Frogs?" Caterwaul asked him. "What frogs?"

"What frogs? . . . You're joking!" The turtle was laughing. "Well then it's a good thing that I just happened to sneeze when I did. Because, my friend, you'd be skewered like a shish kebab before you walked even another fifty feet in the direction you're going."

The cat cocked his head slightly to show that he clearly did not understand.

"Ol' Fairfax is on maneuvers, mate. Haven't seen 'em this riled up in a long time either. This," he said paddling at the water, "is Bug Stool Creek. Everyone knows that Bug Stool Creek is guarded by that blighter general and his army of poison dart frogs."

Just then a high-pitched whizzing sounded above Caterwaul's head. Looking up he saw a sharpened quill, as if from a porcupine or hedgehog, sticking out of a tree trunk.

"Well, they know you're here now mate. Sorry . . . but you're on your own." The turtle dove off his rock and disappeared beneath the water.

Another dart flew by Caterwaul and then another. He ducked down just in time to dodge a fourth dart that actually parted his fur as it sailed over his head.

After that, he took off like a thunderbolt. He could see them, forming ranks all around him. They were everywhere, small frogs, with colorful markings, armed with what he thought looked to be . . . wishbones? Were they actually using bows made out of wishbones?

Whatever they were, they were dangerous. Each of the frogs seemed able to reload and launch a minimum of three or four of the poisoned quills per minute. Caterwaul was in serious trouble. He had to get away . . . now! He pumped his legs faster than he thought possible. There was no way he was going to die here in the mud next to some filthy stream called Bug Stool Creek.

Then he felt one of the barbs pierce his right side. He was terrified. He had no idea what type of poison was on the tip of the arrow. He imagined it was some form of neurotoxin or a muscle inhibitor, like curare or something. He'd often heard that frogs were able to generate toxins within their own skins. A second quarrel hit him in the right hind leg and then a third, in the right shoulder. Still he ran. He was distressed, but he did not dare let up.

Yanking the barbs free of his flesh, he continued to run. Scared as he was, it did not occur to him that the poison appeared ineffective.

Finally, after about half an hour, his legs gave out, not because they were paralyzed, but from sheer exhaustion. Slumped over and gasping for breath, the cat lay trembling, propped up against a dead branch resting on the ground. He was so close to the edge of consciousness that he hardly felt the large reptilian paws lifting him up to carry him away.

~

The sun wasn't down an hour when the rat crawled back up the muddy rocks to the cave entrance. It had started to rain, and he was covered in muck. His coarse, wiry fur jutted out from his body in all directions.

"It's done," he said. "I did it . . . just like you told me to." He was laughing. "I swear I don't think ol' Fairfax has had that much fun in years."

"You made sure to tell the general not to hurt him?"

"Absolutely, ma'am. The frogs were all shooting blanks. If they hit him, all he'd have felt was a little prick. Kind of fitting, if you ask me."

"You are positive? You know what I will do to you if I find that you are not being truthful."

The rat swallowed hard. "Don't worry, ma'am. I swear to you there was no toxin on any of 'em. After all, there's plenty enough frogs out there in this wood already. But if you don't mind my askin' . . . why d'ya let the ungrateful little fur ball go? It doesn't make any sense to me."

The old woman lowered her hood back onto her shoulders. Her hair was matted, and her eyes were red. It was obvious she had been crying.

"Of course it doesn't Edsel," she answered curtly before turning to go back down to her home. "I never expected you to understand."

Part 1

On the Outside

1

Cathoon

Barely an apple's throw from Harsizzle Road stood the castle of Cathoon. It was a dark and empty place, the likes of which you only find in the best of fairy tales. It was the kind of place that no decent sort would ever call home. So, for that reason, it was a good thing that the castle's occupant could never be called decent.

In that bare and chilly place lived Queen Druciah, a heartless creature who took delight in the misery of others. Just the sound of her name brought the tiny hairs to attention on the back of the neck.

Tall and gaunt, it was apparent that she had once been a woman of great beauty. Nearly six feet tall, her body draped in blue velvet finery, she still shone with the glow of power. She moved gracefully and with an elegance fitting her royal position. A golden crown set with only the most precious of jewels rested on her brow, her fading auburn hair tied up in a bun.

Druciah looked down from her perch in the hills, watching her subjects as they came and went. It was harvest time, and the village folk were busy. Farmers and their elder sons took their crops down Harsizzle Road to market, while their wives and children handled much of the daily grind. She wrung her stiffening hands together as she watched them through her spyglass.

Clawing mournfully at her thinning hair, she looked with hate upon the young men who went about their courting of the young and lovely village maids.

This made the queen angrier than anything. Seeing the attention that was lavished on beautiful young girls made her blood boil. It wasn't because she hated them. It was because they diverted the attention that she wanted for herself.

Unfortunately, Druciah was cursed with the sin of vanity. The one thing she hated most was that she was getting old, and seeing all those young men and women together only drove that point home.

Though aging was a natural part of life and the way of the world, the queen could not accept that it was happening to her. Every morning she rose from her bed, knowing that there would be a new wrinkle here or a crow's foot there.

She expected at least one new addition daily. Her once pristine skin was becoming loose and mottled. Small moles appeared where there were none before, and the worst insult of all was the hairs, which seemed to appear as if from out of nowhere. It was these stray hairs, more than anything else, which drove her mad.

It seemed like every day there was a new hair. First, one would show up on her cheek, and then another would sprout from her nose, and the next one from the side of her ear. And heaven forbid if one of the hairs happened to protrude from one of the moles? Well . . . there was really no point in going there . . .

"Why is all of this happening to me?" she shrieked, grabbing her ruby-handled tweezers. With a tug, she plucked the unsightly whisker from her cheek and wept into her hands. It seemed there was nothing she could do to halt the march of hated time.

She sent for the land's best and brightest, offering a fortune to anyone able to create a potion for keeping her young. With their mortars and their pestles they tried out a thousand combinations. She hired astronomers and astrologers, chemists and alchemists, but none could provide her with the answer she lusted for. She just kept getting older and more obsessed.

Soon no amount of white lead and vinegar makeup could hide the wrinkles. Every plant and root was crushed and applied to her face, yet nothing seemed to help. If anything, her skin grew worse from all the applications, becoming chalky and pale. Her hair was dyed with a mixture of saffron and cumin to give it color, but it only made her smell like the inside of her chef's spice cabinet.

Nothing worked at all. There was no earthly element, animal, vegetable, or mineral that could give her what she wanted. Even the most expensive periwigs and fine hairpieces adorned with diamonds could not make her happy.

Despite her compulsive behavior, she was still a powerful woman. Though thin, she had the strong neck of a ballerina, and she held her head up proudly through her queenly ruff. Her eyes were those of fierce determination.

If she had only just accepted the inevitability of time, she would have matured gracefully. And, if she opened her eyes and looked around, she'd have realized that the world around her was aging too. But she couldn't see it, and would not accept it. The constant denial turned her sour.

As a young princess, she was beloved. Everyone in the kingdom talked about her and what a fine ruler she might one day become. She had men and women falling over themselves for the chance to be in the same room with her. Every eligible man in the kingdom desired her hand, but no one was good enough. She'd play childish games matching one suitor against another, all the while having no real interest in either.

She'd found it so amusing to watch people jump at her every beck and call.

The Grand Balls she staged upon becoming queen were among the finest ever conceived. Everyone who was anyone begged to be invited. The castle resonated with music and laughter late into the night. The palace walls were adorned with the most intricate tapestries. Works by the country's most respected painters hung in nearly every room. Intellectuals and men of high creative bent became regular fixtures. Yet if there was one single thing that stuck out among all the fine accoutrements featured at her gala affairs, it was the ornately carved ice sculptures imported from the frozen land of Nordlingen. Anyone fortunate enough to see the ice sculptures came away from the experience amazed. The attention to detail by their creators was astonishing. Scenes from the mythological past came alive in the works of virtuosos. Even the placement of the sculptures was executed with purpose. They were set methodically to take advantage of the lighting of their surroundings, and shone like diamonds from most every viewing angle.

Druciah laughed as she turned her suitors away one by one, prince by prince. The worthy ones who might really have loved her were the first she cast aside. She thought their honesty pathetic and considered them weaklings for their genuine efforts to win her heart.

As the years progressed, the Grand Balls, banquets, and other revels continued, as did the queen's indifference. The stone walls echoed each night with the sharp words of ridicule with which she stabbed at good men who had given her such meager amusement. Eventually her soul began to blacken. With the good men driven off, all that remained were the ones who were motivated by their own personal quest for power, not by love or honest attraction.

She grew bitter and enraged. Whenever she'd look down

from her hill and saw people who were happy, she became furious. How dare they be so happy when she was in misery? So she stopped having the Grand Balls and Great Feasts altogether. Their purpose gone, the brilliantly detailed ice swans of Nordlingen simply melted away.

Every morning she'd wake in a foul humor. It was when she was in moods like this that she turned to the most trusted member of her staff, the commander of her secret police, Chief Constable Warwick Vane Bezel III. It was in Warwick that she found the closest thing to a kindred spirit.

~

The queen became rotten over time, but Warwick was born that way. In fact he came from a long line of scoundrels. When he was a very small child, he'd often fashioned clumps of ice into makeshift magnifying glasses and use the sun's rays to burn insects and start fires. He thought it hilarious to dangle food in front of hungry puppies, only to pull it away and eat it himself.

If one were to look up the definition of the word "degenerate" in Dorian Hamster's Old World Dictionary, there would be one of Warwick Vane Bezel III's baby pictures alongside the word to serve as illustration.

One time, for a laugh, he'd replaced a sleeping old man's wooden leg with a French baguette so that he could watch him fall flat on his face. Oh, how he laughed at that one. He was still laughing when he got out of the Reginald R. Grelnitz youth dungeon a month later.

But his most sinister prank as a child by far had to be the time he led a blind friend to a hornet's nest, handed the boy a stick, and told him that if he hit it hard enough then candy would fall out. When asked later how he could do such a despicable thing, and to a "friend" no less, Warwick Vane Bezel III simply said he wanted to make sure the kid would "always remember his twelfth birthday."

Everyone knew the kid was bad, some said irredeemable, and as he grew into his teens his childish pranks took on a whole new level of meanness.

You could never say, though, that Warwick Vane Bezel III wasn't motivated. In fact, he was probably the most determined man in the kingdom to be bad for badness sake. If there was a list of the world's most horrible people, Warwick was going straight to the top, and he would crush whoever stood in his way.

He enrolled in the Harsizzle Hall of Higher Learning where he received an associate's degree in criminal injustice with a minor in general disorder. His favorite class was in police brutality where the core curriculum consisted of learning how to use someone's compassion and kindness against them on a daily basis. That, and of course, cracking people's kneecaps with a billy club.

He' finished at either the top or the bottom of his class, depending on one's perspective. Warwick Vane Bezel III proved to be a fine student of inhuman nature. These were the qualities that later brought him to the queen's attention. He was just the man she needed to be her enforcer. He was a good-looking brute standing nearly six foot four. He had gray eyes that indicated more than a modest intelligence. His long, black hair draped over the back of his armor, and you could tell he had the makings of a fine soldier, if he wasn't so bloody cruel. Druciah made him the head of her secret police, and through the years he never disappointed her.

Soon he became a deterrent to anyone who might disobey the queen's orders. Often she would send him on raids among the villages. Girls and women who were younger or prettier than the queen were systematically rounded up and deported from Druciah's lands forever.

Around the holidays, Warwick Vane Bezel III would devise

devious schemes to get rid of the homeless and other political undesirables. Once he rounded up seventeen of those he considered human flotsam by setting a trap for people who had been avoiding his vagrancy warrants. He sent out invitations, telling them that there would be a cooked goose, free bread pudding, and fresh cider at Ye Old Mission.

Once they arrived with their empty stomachs, he threw them all in the dungeon at Cathoon, every last one. Even the children were captured. After all, thought the constable, children without parents were a terrible nuisance. Might as well grab them now and prevent them from becoming beggars later on.

The queen's taxes were the most obscene. There was a tax on just about everything, from flour to fowl. Of course Warwick Vane Bezel III profited from this as well. Tax farming, he'd called it. For every collection he made, he skimmed a little off the top for himself. It was all approved by the queen and thus all perfectly legal.

If those high taxes kept the townsfolk close to poverty, the nefarious police commander couldn't care less. He would sometimes burst down the doors of people he suspected of "holding out" on him. He and his goons could enter wherever they wanted with impunity and take whatever he said was owed. For that reason alone, he was the man most of the queen's subjects hated above all others as the wellspring of their misery.

~

The queen delighted in the way her constable responded to her every command. He brought in the money she needed, and kept the people in an almost constant state of terror. What more could a queen want in a brute? It was as though she held a noose around the village's neck with Warwick Vane Bezel III to tighten it whenever she gave the word. She had complete control over everything and everyone and no one could do a thing about it.

As much joy as the constable brought the queen, her aging problem remained. She decided to take up magic to try to find a solution in the world of the arcane. She spent a small fortune in amassing the largest collection of magic books and items she could find.

Once she learned of the existence of a book of magic spells that was rumored to have been compiled by the greatest wizard who'd ever lived. She sent out dozens of her guards to procure it. Finally, it had been discovered in the backroom of one of the booksellers doing business in the village of Mauth. The merchant did not want to part with it for obvious reasons, but Druciah's guards were quite insistent.

The book turned out to be of minor use. There wasn't a single incantation that could slow her aging or restore her beauty. Most of the spells were little more than what Druciah considered parlor tricks, but there were a few she could make use of fairly regularly.

She took particular delight in one of them—a spell that could summon up a swarm of insects. Depending on the variation of a few simple words, Druciah could use it to send a horde of grasshoppers, beetles, or mosquitoes after one of her enemies. Unfortunately, like most spells, using it took up much of her energy, so she only used it on special occasions.

But even using the spell book once in a while had the desired effect of making her people fear her more. After all, it was bad enough to be ruled by an evil queen. It was much worse if that queen had magic at her disposal, too.

2

The Cat Arrives

Considering her demeanor, you would think Queen Druciah was incapable of feeling anything toward any living creature, so it wasn't especially surprising to see her reaction when one night a rather dirty and disheveled black cat was found resting on one of the chairs on her terrace.

"You have no right to be here, you furry vagabond! Remove yourself immediately! Shoo!" the queen said.

The cat barely raised its head and, opening its eyes slowly, said "And I say you have no right to disturb me as I sleep. Go away. We will talk about this in the morning."

Druciah was stunned, for she was used to having her every command obeyed. "How dare you—no one speaks to me that way! Leave now or I will have my guards remove you!" screamed the queen.

But the cat simply turned away. "Your guards?" he harrumphed. "Like your guards could ever catch me? Why, half asleep as I am I could avoid your guards, even if they cared about your orders, which you know they don't." He shifted positions again, stretching fully and turning his head from side to side. "Empty threats are all they are . . . There is nothing you can do to me that can top what I've been through already."

The queen was speechless. She wanted to scream for her

guards, but her tongue felt too large to make the words.

"Anyway, who do you think you are?" asked the cat. "You have no idea who I am, and yet already you judge me. You assume automatically that you don't like me."

He tilted his head to one side and laughed. "Your first instinct is to call your guards and drive me away. I'd have thought that you'd have had enough of that already, considering the only living things still around you are on the payroll."

He looked up at her as if to introduce himself. "I am furry, but I am not a vagabond," he ran his tongue over his paw. "All I need is a bit of grooming, that's all. You know, I'd love to see what you'd look like after twenty days on the run through the dense jungle.

"And without a rest too," he continued. "A good brushing and a few squares under my skin, and I could pass for feline royalty, a companion fit for the Egyptian Pharaohs of old."

This apparently was a bit much for Druciah, who had gotten her wind back. She began to laugh. "You . . . royalty? Don't make me laugh. A companion for the Pharaohs? More likely a companion for plague fleas." Having found her voice, she called to her guards. "We have an unwanted visitor."

Three uniformed guards emerged into the room, one carting a bag made of woven grass. The next ten minutes were an exercise in futility with all three guards stumbling awkwardly about the room unable to capture the animal.

"I thought since this castle was called Cathoon, I would be welcome here. I guess I was wrong," the feline said. "Why are you so determined not to like me?" He made a series of three hops, which accented the incompetence of her guards.

"What if I told you I was an enchanted cat?" he inquired as he artfully dodged the approaching arms of one of the queen's clumsy retainers.

"Enchanted? Really? What powers do you possess?" she

asked him. "I have spells like recipes in a cookbook. What can your enchantments give me that I don't already have?"

The black cat laughed. "Are you serious?" he asked as he leaped from a table to the top of a chest of drawers. "It seems to me that people must not like your recipes at all! How else can you explain the lack of hospitality here? From what I see, most people avoid this place like the plague!" He leaped onto a shelf behind her.

"Oh and for the record . . . plague fleas travel on black rats, not black cats." He jumped again, narrowly avoiding the stumbling guard who almost knocked the queen down. "If you want to avoid catching the plague, a furry friend like me could come in pretty handy."

Druciah countered, "I have no need for a cat. There haven't been any rats around here in ages. No rats nor moles, mice nor voles. My castle is clear of vermin of any kind, unless of course you include present company."

The feline glanced at the stumbling guards, assuming it was they, and not he, she referred to. "No rats!" he exclaimed as he ran across the shoulders of one of the guards. "I am glad to hear that. I am much too valuable an animal to waste my time chasing vermin. Plus they taste terrible, unless, of course, they are prepared by a really gifted chef. As far as I'm concerned, I could go the rest of my life without seeing another rat."

Druciah seemed as though she wanted to say something but the cat continued his rant.

"You ever try to have a conversation with a rat? They have absolutely nothing to talk about. And most of them are just awful people . . . and dirty. You don't want to know about it." He landed delicately on the windowsill. "No grooming habits whatsoever." He took the time to clean his front paws again with a few quick licks.

"And I swear, if I have to hear one more time about which sewers have the best . . . " he jumped again, " . . . selection of wriggly things to eat, I think I will just lose my lunch. You know, a rat will eat some really disgusting things." His eyes flashed widely. "I mean really disgusting!"

The queen was by now starting to show signs of amusement. Whether this was from the things the cat was saying or from the sheer ineptitude of her guards would be hard to say. Nevertheless a smile began to form in the corners of her mouth, and if one listened carefully enough, he might have detected some soft chuckling.

The cat railed on.

"Why I knew this one rat that would never shut up." The cat continued to avoid capture as he spoke. "He just kept yammering on about this, or jabbering on about that . . . and this went on all the time, believe me, all the time. It got so bad that I had to sneak around the cavern on tiptoes just so he wouldn't notice me. It was important that I not be seen because, if the rat caught even a sight of this bushy tail, it was over. The next three hours of my life would be booked up instantly and that, my queen, was time I'd never be able to get back.

"Sometimes he'd wake me up in the morning just to tell me that he couldn't sleep. Can you believe it? And he never felt bad about it either. It was like somehow he had the right to wake me up to keep him company. From the way he tells it, he was some kind of bigwig at one time. Rats," he sighed. "No thank you, I don't need 'em."

By now the queen's brief flirtation with amusement had faded, and she became extremely aggravated. "What is wrong with you guards? It's just a cat . . . and an overly talkative one at that. Just grab him quickly and get him out of my castle. I can't believe that I have such inept guards. You can't even capture a little cat!"

Despite his impressive display of catrobatics, the queen's quarry calmly said, "I don't understand you, queen. You live here all alone in this enormous cold castle of stone. I would think you would go insane. It's so cold and empty, and it has no soul. You have no one to talk to."

The queen looked at her guards as if to say *I have them*, but the cat shook his head. "They don't count. You don't talk to them; you give them orders. The only people you allow around you are your guards and servants, and from what I see, they seem to stay here more out of fear than loyalty." He jumped again. "It must be terribly lonely for you, being here in this huge and empty place. I'd think that by now you would be tired of being lonely and that you would welcome a furry little diversion like me."

Druciah stiffened, more upset by the cat's insight than anything else. "You, Sir Cat, know nothing about me, though you seem to consider yourself an expert." Still she turned away. What he'd said obviously struck a nerve.

The guards kept grabbing at him, catching only thin air. It was quite comical they way they thrust and stumbled in pursuit of the wise and unwelcome animal. But then the cat saw the queen was visibly shaken and decided to end the game.

He propelled himself forward and came to rest gently on a table directly in front of her. "My name is Caterwaul," he said. "I will share my wisdom with you if you let me stay with you here in the castle." Tired of the chase, he bowed his head to show respect.

Staring upward at Druciah with his big yellow eyes, he added, "Look . . . I need a place to live and you need a friend. So what do you say? Do you want to give it a try?"

The queen appeared to be sniffling, as if fighting back tears, when she said, "Well I must admit, good Sir Cat, you are a feisty one." She rubbed her chin in consideration. Just then the guard with the woven grass sack dove toward the cat and captured him.

"I have him your majesty," said the guard triumphantly, "I have him!" The guard was grinning from ear to ear. He considered it quite an accomplishment to have been able to finally put that cat in his trap. He was so pleased with himself, he appeared to be dancing; but when he checked the contents of the bag, it was empty. The cat was gone.

By some trick, Caterwaul now sat perched on Druciah's left shoulder. Gliding around her neck, he leaned forward gracefully and whispered in her ear. "I told you I was an enchanted cat."

3

Life in the Castle

Caterwaul settled right in and within a short time became a fixture in the castle. Wherever Druciah went, her black-furred companion followed close behind. When she was sitting, he would curl up at her feet and just rest like he had had not slept in years. They soon became very good friends.

Caterwaul had been right. Druciah, after all those years of loneliness, really needed someone to talk to. The cat showed he was a good listener and counselor too. Before long, they were inseparable. He found that he liked doing the things she liked. If the queen wanted to read, then Caterwaul would read as well. Usually he could be found curled up on a pillow next to her or, at most, only a few feet away.

But what he really loved to do was play games, and she proved to be a competent and enthusiastic opponent. For hours on end they would play. Often it was card games with names like penguins, tiger's eye, or three crowns. More often than not, it was Caterwaul who was victorious.

Sometimes if they fancied a longer game, they'd invite Warwick Vane Bezel III and one of the guards for a tournament. With four of them playing, they might indulge themselves with an adventurous game of "One and Thirty." Caterwaul loved it when Warwick joined in. He took special delight in watching the commander's brow furrow whenever he would fall behind. And since in these games, for Warwick, losing was a regular event, his face often looked like a shriveled apple left too long in the sun.

Of course losing did not sit well with a man like Warwick Vane Bezel III. He had a terrible temper. The secret policeman's hatred for Caterwaul grew with every defeat. Warwick knew the cat was laughing at him, and he did not like it one bit.

These tournaments could and often did extend deep into the night. They would sometimes lose track of time and only realize how long they had been playing when the light in the oil lamps began to fade.

Caterwaul liked other kinds of games as well. He was especially fond of board games, which required strategy. When he lived back in the forest, he and the Witch would spend hours upon hours trying to outmaneuver each other. One day he approached his new mistress with a query. "How would you like to see me move castles?" he asked.

She stared at him incredulously. "Surely that is not within your power. You cannot actually move my castle from one place to another?"

He smiled and said, "Of course not, my queen. I was just asking you if you might be interested in having a game of chess."

~

Warwick Vane Bezel III had a long history of hating animals. One could not help but notice this, considering he had spent most of his life torturing and subjecting them to all sorts of cruelties. He really didn't like much of anything, but animals were high on his list of things he didn't like. Oh . . . and animals who were smarter than he was, he hated most of all.

It did not matter if the beast was enchanted or not, or that Queen Druciah was obviously fond of him. Warwick Vane Bezel III considered Caterwaul the castle's lowest occupant. He was always spying on the queen's new companion. He did not trust him at all and was determined to catch him doing something disloyal, which he could show the queen.

But Caterwaul was loyal, and after months living together in the castle, he and the queen were quite attached. Where the queen went, Caterwaul followed. And there was no doubt that he had a mellowing effect on her personality. Unfortunately it would never last long. Some sign of happiness from the villagers below or a bit of news from some far off corner of the kingdom would bring back her bitterness.

This time, it was a wedding announcement that knocked her out of balance. It was brought to her by royal courier one cold Thursday afternoon. It was no more than a few lines on a bit of parchment. It seemed one of her former courtiers, Count Mikhail Freeholder, was getting married in three days' time. This bit of news should not have surprised her, for the count had been one of her more enthusiastic pursuers, but he was also one of the most worthless.

Count Mikhail Freeholder was looking to catch himself a wealthy wife. Though he was an aristocrat by birth, he didn't have two coins to rub together, and the queen knew it. In fact, her pet name for him was "Count Freeloader." She was never remotely interested in him, other than as the butt of a joke.

But that was before the suitors disappeared. It had been years since any man had called on her, and now, even this Freeloader's attentions would be welcome.

"So the count is getting married," she said aloud to herself. Not if Druciah could help it!

"Warwick!" she shouted to the commander of her secret police. "I have a job for you."

Warwick Vane Bezel III snapped to attention. "What is it you want me to do, your majesty?"

"Count Freeholder thinks he is getting married next week. I want you to find out who is providing the nuptial feast. Tell him that he will no longer be needed, because Queen Druciah wants to provide the catering for the whole affair." She laughed evilly. "It is, after all, the least I can do for my old friend, Freeloader."

She tossed him a pouch of coins. "Give the caterer this for his troubles, then find out whoever is making the bride's dress, and tell him that we won't be needing him either." She spun around laughing, impressed with her genius. She handed him a piece of paper with instructions on it. "Make sure that you drop this off with our royal seamstress. Tell her that it's a gift for our future countess. I want it made to those measurements exactly and those exact color specifications. And she needs to be quick about it. Time is of the essence. I will need it in two days."

"Oh, and Warwick," she added, "on your way out, tell Orris, my chef, that I need to see him now." She smiled and giggled with evil delight. "As I recall the count is deathly allergic to eggs."

~

Orris, the royal chef, had been in the queen's service for many years. Talented and devoted, he was the creative force behind the queen's Great Feasts and was unmatched in his skillful use of cutlery and seasonings. There wasn't a dish you could name that Orris had not perfected. If it swam in the sea, flew through the air, grew or grazed in the field, the queen's man knew how to prepare it.

Like most men of considerable ability, Orris had a rather large ego. Nothing got the fires going in him like the challenge of putting together a great feast. He likened himself to a great composer, only rather than musical notes, his medium was food. He and his dozen or so assistants would regularly prepare masterpieces of delectability and the kitchen would resound with the aromas of his savory symphonies.

Breads and pastries were his personal favorites to work with. He was a genius when it came to creating new recipes for cakes and pies. And if you were among those lucky enough to have sampled his mouthwatering lemon almond soufflé, you could expect to die a happy man. He used to boast that he could bake anything blindfolded and with one arm tied behind his back. Unfortunately in recent years, he'd had dwindling opportunities to practice his craft. There had not been a Grand Ball or a Great Feast in a very long time.

Still like most performers, Orris needed to perform. If he could not display his talents for the Harsizzle elite, he would have to make do with what audience was available. These days, the audience for his presentations usually consisted of Warwick Vane Bezel III and a few of his henchmen. Oh well . . . what they may have lacked in discriminating palates was more than made up for by their complete absence of table manners.

Then of course, there was the queen herself. Though her appetite for fanciful parties was gone, she still was able to offer Orris regular challenges. Unfortunately, more often than not, these were designed not to delight her subjects, but to cause them misery.

The chef knew his talents were being wasted, but he dared not say anything out of fear that his predecessor's fate might befall him as well. Orris remembered how Elias, the queen's last personal chef, was confined to the castle's dungeon for months because the queen found a hair in her shepherd's pie.

Even thinking about it caused him to become uneasy. Orris, who was but an assistant at the time, recalled Elias arguing with the queen over whose hair it was that was in the pie. The argument was pointless because no matter which of them was right, the cook was doomed either way.

The former chef sealed his fate when he pointed out that the small piece of meat to which the hair was attached looked suspiciously like a mole that had, until only moments before, been twitching on the queen's upper lip.

Orris would not make that or any other mistake, so he kept his mouth shut and his kitchen spotless. Since he didn't have much to prepare, he spent his time scrubbing, polishing, and sanitizing most of the day. He was in the midst of this cleaning when he received the queen's summons. Druciah was grinning ear to ear when her chef approached.

"You wanted to see me, my queen?"

"Yes, Orris," she said, "I have a special challenge for you. One I think will enable you to exercise your culinary muscles and test your creativity."

"Are we going to have a Grand Ball this year, your highness?" asked Orris excitedly.

"No, you fool. Those days are long past, I'm afraid, but I said I had a challenge for you and I think this is one you will appreciate. I need you to assemble every recipe you have containing eggs. We are catering a wedding in three days."

She was absolutely giddy as she gave Orris his instructions.

"We shall spare no expense. I want you to really stretch out creatively here. You are going to make the most elaborate and decorative dishes you can come up with. I don't care what you create, my friend, just make sure that whatever you cook contains eggs.

"I even want the side dishes and desserts to have eggs in them. Get started now and have them ready by the morning of the third day. Then when you're done, have the whole lot delivered to Count Freeholder for his wedding reception."

~

Two days later, Secret Police Commander Warwick Vane Bezel III returned to the castle. He had followed the queen's orders to the letter. "The caterers have been paid off, and your seamstress has completed the dress you asked for. And if you don't mind my saying so, I believe that she really outdid herself this time. I am afraid, however, that I made the dress quite a mess, your majesty." He handed her what appeared to be an orange circus tent adorned with bright circles of purple and green. "I was going to surprise you by having my horse wear it for the journey home, but he refused to allow me to get on his back. It was quite embarrassing to the steed."

"Excellent work, Warwick! I knew I could count on you!" She unfolded the dress, which was designed to make the wearer look like an oversized, human Easter egg. She burst out laughing. "Yes, Warwick, this is perfect . . . In this outfit our bride-to-be will look like a cross between a clown and Humpty Dumpty. I think it goes perfectly with our theme for the day." She broke into a roar.

After she had time to compose herself, she asked, "What other mischief did you get into on your visit to the village? You know how much I love to hear of your adventures."

"Well, I don't mean to brag, your highness, but I took a bit of liberty in giving the bride a new hairstyle. It's a bit radical, but I trust that your majesty will approve," said the commander with an evil grin.

"Oh?" she inquired. "And what new coiffure did you leave her with? A bouffant, a beehive, a flattop, or worse? A Mohawk perhaps?"

"None of the above, my queen," he said with a laugh. "I am afraid my cosmetological skills leave something to be desired. I couldn't decide what to do, so I just took it all." He tossed her a leather bag. She reached inside and pulled out several handfuls of long, red hair.

She was positively giddy. "Excellent! Now she will really look like an egg! My dear Warwick, you really are a devil. I'm afraid that the count and his fiancée are really going to have to 'scramble' if they are to have any hope whatsoever of saving this wedding."

4

Vanity's Curse

"I hate these mirrors!" the queen shouted one morning. She hurried across the room from her mirror to a bookshelf.

"What is it, my queen?" asked the cat.

"Why is it that every day when I look at one of those wretched things, the only things I see are more wrinkles and furrows and unwanted hairs in unwanted places?" She took a book of magic spells from the bookshelf and thumbed through its contents. She threw it down and grabbed another, and yet another after that.

"Nothing!" she wailed dejectedly. "None of my books have even one spell to slow the aging process, much less anything to restore my former youth and beauty."

"Well, of course not, your majesty," the cat retorted. "To do that would require some heavy-duty magic, a magic of the black variety, if you know what I mean. In order to turn back the hands of time and restore you to the way you once were would require access to the kind of magic that only a very powerful witch or wizard would possess."

"Why Caterwaul, my love, you were once enthralled to a witch. You told me yourself that while you were with her you learned quite a bit of magic. Do you possess the necessary skills to restore my lost beauty?"

"I am afraid not, my queen," he said. "That kind of mischief is way out of my league. Even if I did have that kind of power, I would be afraid to use it. Trust me. There are some forces in this world that are just not worth trifling with."

"A pity," she lamented, "because I would give anything, perhaps even my entire kingdom, to possess that knowledge." She stroked Caterwaul's fur, and the cat purred contentedly. "Take you, for example. You are a cat and you are beautiful and you will keep hold of that beauty for nine lives.

"If only there was a spell that could give me that kind of beauty and longevity. Just imagine that, Caterwaul. How wonderful would it be if I, Druciah, could rule the land for nine lifetimes, the most beautiful and powerful of queens ever to walk the earth? I would be virtually immortal."

Caterwaul briefly considered explaining to her that the whole "nine-lives" thing was actually more of an expression than something to be taken literally, but then he thought better of it. She was in a terrible mood, and there was no use in upsetting her further.

"Oh, why can't I be beautiful again, my pet? I really would give anything to not have to see what I've become every time I look in a mirror. Is there anything that you can do, anything at all to help me?"

"Well," he said joking, "I suppose I could put a curse on all the castle's mirrors. We could make it a curse that would turn you from a human into something else—perhaps a cat like me, or something silly like that—if you glanced into one. That would make you think twice before looking at a mirror, wouldn't it? Ha ha, wouldn't it?" He repeated, laughing.

The queen looked at him, and he could tell that, though he had only been joking around, she was seriously considering this. "You could do this for me?" she asked. "Oh Caterwaul, if you will do this for me, I will share the castle with you."

"Share the . . . the castle? You mean to say that this huge

castle would be partly mine?" He could not believe his ears.

"You would like that wouldn't you, Caterwaul? I mean we share it right now, don't we? You are my only true friend in the world. My life has become so much more enjoyable since you first arrived. Why not make it official? Wouldn't that be wonderful?"

She went on. "You could remake half the castle in your image. Design it to what you think cats would enjoy. And then you could invite your new cat friends over to enjoy it with us. I do so much prefer the company of cats to that of dreary old humans."

"Yes, of course . . ." Caterwaul stammered, surprised. "I mean, I suppose I could. But why would you want me to do it? I mean, aren't there enough unwanted cats in the world already? The sudden appearance of more could create a lot of problems. Who would take care of them all?

"And what if you were to forget that all of the mirrors were cursed, and you accidentally looked into one? You don't really think that you would be happy as a cat? Do you, my queen?"

But the wheels were already turning inside her corrupt mind. "Oh don't worry, my dear. If there is a sudden rise in the feline population, things won't be so bad. The people who remain will just have to take care of them. And they will, Caterwaul, because now the cats will literally be part of their family. And those cats that don't have someone to love them can come live here with us in the castle. We have more than enough room here at Castle Cathoon. Oh Caterwaul, it will be a paradise." She was positively beaming.

"But remember my beloved pet, it must be every single mirror in my kingdom; you have to curse them all."

Druciah chuckled—no, it was more of a cackle of delight.

She thought to herself: every time that a beautiful young girl and a handsome man even glanced at a mirror, they will be transformed. Pretty soon, there will be cats everywhere, and people will wonder what happened to all of their loved ones. Eventually, the people will catch on and they will smash every mirror in the kingdom, but by then the damage will be done.

"Oh vanity, thy name is Kitty," she whispered as she turned her mirror around to face the wall.

"I imagine the mouse population will suffer some," Caterwaul joked, not really expecting any kind of response. And it was a good thing he was being rhetorical, because the queen was far away, lost in her own thoughts.

"Druciah, my queen," Caterwaul became serious again. "Just assume that I can do this for you, my dear friend. You know that it really isn't going to solve the root problem here. You are going to continue getting older. It's a part of nature, and because of this, it's unfortunately unavoidable. Unless . . ." his voice trailed off as he was thinking.

The cat jumped from his resting place and took a seat beside Druciah on the couch. She rubbed the top of his head with her nails the way he liked it.

"You said *unless . . .*" she said, continuing the head massage.

He purred ecstatically as if to say *don't stop, that feels wonderful.*

"Please, by all means continue my pet."

He leaned his head back. This was very satisfying, he thought, and then he continued. "As I have said many times, my queen, my powers are limited. However, during my time spent living with the Witch of Red Moon Forest, I learned that there may be a way to bring back your youth." He stretched his whole body contentedly.

He continued, "Performing anything as bold as this requires black magic, and black magic usually comes with a heavy price. But the Witch of Red Moon Forest is well-versed in the forbidden arts. As far as I can recall, she retains in her cave a collection of spells that can lead to the creation of a confection that just might be what you're looking for." The words flowed from his mouth like a song.

He shifted his position and spoke earnestly, "But I don't know if she will even see you, much less agree to help you." Druciah stroked his back delicately, running her long, bony fingers from his shoulders all the way to the end of his bushy, black tail.

"And even getting to her is going to be a challenge. It will take you many days, perhaps even a week or more, just to reach Red Moon Forest. Then once you're there, you will have to find the entrance. I would wait for nightfall before going in."

He waited for her to resume his massage before continuing his instructions. "Once inside the forest, you'll see a path that has seen scant use in recent years. It's become a little bit overgrown. If you stay on this path, you soon will learn that there are three perils, which you must endure.

"First you must gain the respect of the Parliament of Possums, who can be a real pain in the hindquarters. They're marsupials, you see. They think that it's their job to make the laws of the forest, and the Witch is happy to let them go right on thinking it.

"But they're just your typical politicians. They look all high and mighty, but get next to nothing done. Let me tell you, the only thing worse than a politician is a politician with a pouch. I never liked possums much, with their white faces and pink noses; they think they're so important. Possums . . . rats in trees are more like it." He realized he was going off on a tangent.

"But you can't kill them. So you will have to make that especially clear to your guards. No matter how much they frustrate you, don't make any hostile moves, or you might as well just come right back home. You need them. Only they can guide you to the next challenge.

"Now this second peril is far more difficult. If the possums trust you, they will send you down along a trail, which will take you to an enormous, hollow oak tree. The tree is massive, so there is no way you can miss it as long as you follow the right trail.

"Once you get there you will have to be extra careful, because inside that tree lives a very large and eccentric snapping turtle named Joffrey, who is extremely dangerous. He is quite a neat freak, and he hates visitors. If you disrupt a single leaf or disturb even one stone, he will snap you in half. He fancies himself quite the decorator, so keep that in mind." Caterwaul again started to go off on a tangent. "He's actually very good though . . . I've learned a few things about décor from him myself.

"Finally, you will have to deal with the poison dart frogs of Bug Stool Creek. If you can figure out a way to get by them, then you can follow the creek bed about half a kilometer, and this will lead you to the cave the Witch calls home. If she agrees to see you, you may be able to make a deal, but again I can offer you no guarantees."

The cat licked his paw. "There will probably be some other unanticipated dangers you will come across too. So if you are going, make sure to take at least four of your best guards with you for protection, smart ones if you can find them.

"Be sure that you take that animal Warwick Vane Bezel III with you too. He just might come in handy if you find yourself in a pickle. But remember, guys like that can get you killed, so make sure he keeps his mouth shut and his eyes open.

"I'll be here when you get back." He curled up on a pillow as if to go to sleep.

"You mean you will not go with me?" asked the queen.

"Absolutely not!" he declared. "That forest is dangerous. I

was only able to escape before because I had learned enough magic to do so. It is going to take you many days before you even get to the forest. So of course, I'm staying here. As far as I'm concerned, one trip through the Forest of Red Moon is enough for a lifetime, or even nine.

"Besides, if I am able to pull off this 'cursed mirror' spell for you, it's going to wipe me out. I'm just a cat, so I'm small. Performing any kind of real magic takes a toll on the user. I've been unconscious for days after performing relatively minor incantations. Something this big will likely put me out for a week or more. If you want the mirrors cursed, then I will be staying here."

Druciah agreed. "Okay, cat. You can stay behind. But before you get too comfortable, you need to know that by tonight I expect every mirror in the kingdom to be turning people into cats.

"In fact," she said, "why not start with this one here? It will be a test to see how much you learned from that Witch. No use setting off on a long journey unless I know the end prize is obtainable."

Caterwaul's whiskers twitched as he silently mouthed an incantation. The queen squinted to try to see what it was he said, but was unable to transpose the cat's lip movements. It was obvious, though, that the spell was siphoning away his energy.

The queen turned the surface of the mirror toward the door and called for one of her guards. As soon as he came within sight of the mirror, he saw his reflection and instantly transformed into a small gray cat.

"Excellent," she laughed elatedly and clapped her hands. "I guess that means I'm off to see the Witch." She obscured the mirror with a silken red cover.

"When I get back, you can release the spell, but let's have a little fun for a while." As she left the room, she was practically skipping, the way little girls sometimes do. She called back to Caterwaul, "Remember to do something with all the palace mirrors before you cast your spell. I don't want to come home to a castle full of cats."

Caterwaul could hear her wild laughter echoing through the castle halls.

5

The Parliament of Possums

With the ferocity of a flash flood the queen and her guards set off along the road to the Red Moon Forest to seek out the Witch who lived there. All in all, there were seven in her entourage. The queen rode in her carriage with her driver while four of her most capable underlings rode on horses out in front. Bringing up the rear was the always-wary secret police commander, Warwick Vane Bezel III. Just setting out on this journey was quite an undertaking. It was exhausting for the aging queen, who had not left the castle for years.

The trip was made even more difficult by the fact that as they traveled, there was no one around to offer them hospitality. They rode through several villages and hamlets, and not one person came out to greet them or offer them any assistance. No innkeeper offered them lodging, and no stable boys emerged to feed their horses. It was as if word had spread that the hated queen was on the road, and everybody had run away in fear.

The public's reaction wasn't really that surprising, since the queen almost never left Cathoon Castle. The fact that she was out among them now, and that the hated Warwick Vane Bezel III was with her too, made the people of her kingdom feel uneasy. Having the head of any secret police force in tow rarely makes for adoring citizens.

But this lack of fanfare was little matter to Druciah and her retainers. If they needed to rest they simply stopped and occupied whatever abandoned home struck their fancy. Every so often, they would find a home where the residents had not been gone for too long, and because of this, their homes and stores were quite well-provisioned.

Still, she thought, it would have been nice to actually see some other faces besides Warwick and the other guards.

~

After more than two weeks on the road, the party reached the edge of Red Moon Forest. Her heart sank. Obviously the queen was not prepared to encounter something so vast. The untamed wilderness seemed to extend in either direction as far as the eye could see, and she knew in her heart it was likely as deep as it was wide.

She called to her driver, screaming, "Halt the beasts; we're here!" The coach pulled to a stop, and the queen stepped out of her carriage to look around. "Warwick! I need you to find the best way for us to enter this place. Take two of the guards and ride north. Have the other guards ride south. If neither group finds a way in within the next few hours, turn around and come back."

"But what if we do find a way in, your majesty?" asked one of her more intelligent guards.

Shaking her head dumbfounded, Druciah answered. "Well, I suppose then you will come back immediately and let the rest of us know where it is . . . won't you?"

The guards split up and rode off in opposite directions. It was nearly four hours before Warwick Vane Bezel III and his party returned. Sending one of his riders south to retrieve the others, the commander dismounted and approached the queen's carriage.

"Your majesty, I believe I have spotted a place that looks like it might be a possible entrance. It's about an hour north of here. However, my guards and I explored the area, and I must tell you, this is a very difficult wood. This forest is not going to be passed through easily. If we go in at all, it's going to have to be on foot."

From Caterwaul's directions Druciah had expected this would be no light undertaking, but she didn't realize the wood would be so dense that they would have to fight their way through it. Then it dawned on her: Caterwaul would have seen things through his cat eyes; the forest would be far easier for one of his size to pass than it would be for a human.

As soon as the other three guards returned, the party turned north and rode to where Warwick Vane Bezel III had seen the likely entrance point. Immediately the queen knew that her secret police commander had failed utterly to communicate the fullness of the forest's growth.

"On foot indeed," she said. "Warwick, you idiot!" she bellowed. "What impassable thicket have you brought me to? This is no entrance! We would need fifty men with axes and torches to be able to get through this tangle."

"My apologies your majesty," answered Warwick Vane Bezel III, "but you'll remember I said that it would be difficult. And of all the places we checked out, this was by far the most suitable place to try to go in."

Druciah sat down on a stump to think. She was sure there was no way to make it into the woods through this entrance where they now stood. She felt disappointed; her quest to find the Witch of Red Moon Forest might be over before it really had a chance to begin.

Just then, she noticed a darkening of the sky. The sun had begun to drop below the tree line. As it disappeared from sight, strange slithering noises began emanating from the woods. They all turned in order to see what was happening. What they heard was unnatural. It sounded as though something, or a great many somethings, were being dragged along the forest floor.

Then she remembered Caterwaul's words that she should wait until nightfall before entering the forest. As the sky grew darker Druciah could see the thick growth of Red Moon Forest was retreating. Soon it had pulled back enough to reveal an obvious path. It was still impossible for them to use the horses, but it was now easily passable for a small party on foot.

"All right, everyone. It looks like we're going to have to walk from here," barked Warwick Vane Bezel III. He was a man used to command. "Gather all of our supplies and weapons. We're going into unknown territory. We have no idea what to expect other than that we will have sorcery and a lot of strange animals to deal with."

"Is this place haunted?" one of the guards asked.

"If it's not haunted, it is certainly dangerous," the commander answered. "I expect some of us may not survive. But that doesn't matter, as long as your queen is safe."

"Your sacrifices are, of course, appreciated," added the queen, with a sardonic grin.

The Red Moon Forest had been the setting for many tales of the supernatural. For generations these tales had entertained and frightened people of all stripes throughout the kingdom, from beggars to nobles. Now here was Queen Druciah, standing at the entrance, gazing down the pathway that would soon bring her face to face with the legendary Parliament of Possums.

The guards whispered to one another, as if giving each other last rites. Leaving one of the guards behind with the queen's carriage and its driver, the party stepped into the unknown. Two of the guards carried between them a large, intricately carved chest made of cedar wood.

"Let's go!" Druciah barked condescendingly. "I can't believe what pathetic guards I have. All of you keep your eyes and ears open at all times. And whatever you do, do not drop that cedar chest," she said. "If anything happens to that box we are all finished, do you understand me?" The group nodded in unison and moved slowly along the pathway into the forest.

"Your Highness, I'll go first," Warwick volunteered. "There is no danger that I am afraid to face and no animal that I'm unwilling to eat. There is no spook or specter alive or dead that I will not willingly confront to defend your majesty."

"Thank you, Warwick. Sometimes it's nice to see a little backbone. You may proceed," the queen said. "But be careful. I do not want us to make any enemies out of creatures we may need to use for our gain."

Warwick Vane Bezel III took up the lead position, followed by the rest of the party. The forest was a whole lot spookier than any of them had expected. They followed the path and soon entered a part of the wood that could almost be called a swamp. It was dark and wet and reeked of many unpleasant things, which they'd often smell as the wind shifted directions. However, as terrible and foul as the odors were, the group was far more unsettled by the continuous barrage of strange and eerie sounds echoing through the trees.

They traveled the path through the marsh for most of a day, not really knowing in which direction they were headed, when they finally came to a clearing. As this was the first clear, dry area they'd come across in a while not crawling with worms, bugs and other nasty lurking things, Druciah gave the order to stop. "We will camp here for the night."

"Camp here?" came a voice from above. "You most certainly will not camp here. Can't you see that Parliament is in session?"

The queen looked up to see, hanging upside down from the tree limbs, quite a large gathering of possums. Each of them had on a stark-white, powdered wig secured to its gray and black ears with tiny straps, and they all wore long, black robes which, considering most of the possums hung upside down, appeared to cover nothing.

The queen shielded her eyes. "Parliament indeed. What sort of Parliament goes about exposing themselves to unsuspecting people who accidently wander into their midst? You wear such beautiful wigs, and robes of state. Are you telling me that none among you has ever heard of undergarments? Come down from those trees at once! There is a lady present, and all of you are positively indecent!" exclaimed the queen.

Embarrassed at the offense they had caused, the possums all quietly scurried down the tree trunks to the ground.

"We are sorry, madam . . . we are not used to the presence a lady, or any humans for that matter, around here," said one of the possums as the others tried to present themselves respectably. "We are the Parliament of Possums, and we are the government in this part of the forest."

The possums surrounded them as Warwick unsheathed his sword. Queen Druciah watched as the group of marsupials melted into what appeared to be little chairs filling a great open hall. The animals began to mutter amongst themselves in Possumese.

"If you do anything to us, you will be lost in this forest forever . . . so I suggest you place that carving tool back where it was and show us some respect! I am Prime Minister Pickford, and I need to know why you are here. I need to be sure that you are not here to exploit the raw materials of this forest," he said. "You could say we are environmentalists. We protect this great unspoiled land. You humans have a habit of destroying places like this. You like to call it progress, I believe.

"This Parliament has been formed to protect this land from being ravaged by the likes of you. Your kind mines for minerals and leaves the landscape bare and burning. You chop down trees and destroy whole communities of animals so that you can have more space. You are always looking for more space to live in. You are monsters."

He found a tree limb, which was especially close to the queen's face and scurried onto it. "It is all done for your own greed. You are the most selfish of species. My brethren and I would sooner see you as fodder for the vultures than help you to chop down even one tree. Everything in this forest is precious to us, and nothing may leave except by choice. Now if you understand me, speak," said Pickford. He rose up on his hind legs to his full and massive height of two feet and three inches. "Now be truthful because the Parliament of Possums has ways to know if you speak the truth."

The queen spoke, surprisingly humbly, "Mr. Prime Minister . . . if that is the correct protocol for addressing such an august personage . . . or rather I should say 'possumage' . . . I assure you, I have all the wealth that I will ever need. Though we obviously caught you in the midst of important deliberations, I swear to you that we did not intend to disturb you or anything within this great and noble forest.

"My business is with the Witch, who is reported to live in these parts. That is the only reason I am here. If you could just point me in the right direction, we will be off and out of your affairs forever. I am sure you don't want us 'hanging around' here any longer than absolutely necessary," the queen giggled.

"The Witch, you say? Not rocks nor trees nor water source? Why should I believe you when so many of your kind have lied in the past? Well, there is no way for me to know for certain if you are telling me the truth."

Just then a young, female possum in the third row spoke up. "Point of order, Mr. Prime Minister." The possum's name was Patience, and she was being considered as a possible future replacement for Pickford, who was her uncle.

"There is a way of knowing whether or not she speaks true.

It is an old method, and granted, one that we don't like to use today, civilized society and all, but there is a way; and I will volunteer to administer the test, if no one else will."

Hushed whispers flew around the clearing through the Parliament's membership. The test was foolproof, but it was also very dangerous to the possum that performed it.

Pickford turned to the Parliament of Possums. "Is there anyone else here among the Parliament who would volunteer to perform this procedure?" There was silence. "Patience, very well, you may proceed."

Patience came forward and sat on a stump before the queen. "Stick your hand in my pouch. By the trembling of your hand, I will know if you speak the truth. If you are lying to me, I will know this too. And for any deception you will be sent away from here, and neither you nor your men will ever find your way out of the forest. Are we in agreement?"

"We are agreed," said the queen.

Druciah slowly slipped her hand in the possum's pouch as Patience began to snicker. "That tickles . . . ooh and it's cold too." The queen kept her hand in the possum's pouch for what must have been a full two minutes. She remained completely motionless for the entire time. Patience then indicated to the queen that she could remove her hand, and Druciah withdrew very slowly.

"It's okay, Mr. Prime Minister," said the young possum. "She is being truthful."

Prime Minister Pickford swung around on his tree limb and dropped to the ground, where he replaced his niece on the stump before the queen. "Very well," he said, "we will have a vote. All possums in favor in telling her the way to go, say aye!" When the vote was called, it seemed unanimous. The Parliament agreed to help Druciah on her way.

"Alright, miss, this is what you will do. Head west from this clearing until you come to a massive oak, and from there head south towards Bug Stool Creek." Pickford paused there as if to gather his thoughts before continuing. "But I warn you, and this is extremely important, so you must listen well. When you near the area with the oak tree, you should take special care not to disturb the layout anywhere close to the tree.

"If you should leave so much as a branch or stone disturbed, you will have a very large and angry turtle to deal with. And when I say large, I do not even begin to properly represent this reptile. This turtle's head alone is so large it is capable of snapping a man in half with a single bite. When you come near him, you will see what I mean. And while you are there, make sure you pick up your trash."

"Thank you, Sir Pickford, for all your help," said the queen. "We will take your advice to heart." Then the queen turned to speak with Patience. "I just wanted to say to you, my young possum, that you acted very bravely, especially considering your condition."

The Parliament did not know what the queen was talking about. Druciah continued, "When my hand was in your pouch I could feel your babies kicking. I imagine that it will only be a few more days until you will need that pouch for more than just detecting lies. If I were you, I would be expecting at least four or five new family members."

The party spent the night feasting with the possums. The next morning, they rose to continue their journey.

While the Queen's Away the Cat Will Play

Queen Druciah was in excessively high spirits while she prepared for her journey to see the Witch. Caterwaul had done his part. The spell was cast, cursing all of the mirrors in Harsizzle. If anyone dared to look into one, they instantly became a cat. Most of the people who owned mirrors smashed them shortly after seeing what was happening to their loved ones. If Druciah had not been en route to the forest, she undoubtedly would have found it all quite hilarious.

Since he had done what she asked of him, Druciah kept her promise and allowed the cat to stay behind in the castle. She could hardly have done otherwise, as he was unconscious and likely to remain that way for several days at least.

The queen had been so pleased with him in fact, that her last words to her staff were, "If you need anything done, see Caterwaul. I am leaving him in charge."

As she and her party had ridden away, she'd smiled at the sight of all of the new cats that had already taken up residence in her lands.

If she had given it any real thought whatsoever, Druciah probably would have liked it better had she not added the part about Caterwaul being "in charge," because once he regained consciousness, Caterwaul took it to heart. The way he looked at things, if he really was in charge, he was going to do things his way. You see, Caterwaul assumed that the queen and her party would fail. He knew what the forest was like, and he assumed that the queen would come running home before she got even fifty yards into the woods. Therefore, if she did not return within two weeks, he would assume it was because she couldn't and had been killed by some forest peril.

After two weeks and a couple of days had passed, the cat was sure they were all dead. That meant, or at least he assumed so, that Castle Cathoon was his to do with as he liked. Ever since he had arrived, he'd been dropping hints to the queen about redecorating at least part of the palace. Plus most everyone on staff heard that she had made him her heir. Now it was his chance to go all the way.

He was sad that the queen had to die for him to get this chance. But such was life. If he had to wager on which of the perils got the travelers, he would have guessed Joffrey. That crazy Joffrey was always a snap-first-and-ask- questions-later kind of turtle. He kind of liked the idea of Warwick Vane Bezel III becoming turtle food, but not his friend, the queen.

Nevertheless, it was now more than a month since they'd set out and they were all dead to his mind. To a cat, a month was an eternity. There was no use in wasting valuable time grieving. He had brick masons coming over in the afternoon to build him a nice low bridge overlooking the brand new koi pond he had installed the day before. If there was one thing that Caterwaul really enjoyed, it was popping a big, ugly goldfish in the face with his paw.

Pretty soon, most of the castle's residents were also convinced that the queen was dead and that Caterwaul was now the new master of the kingdom. He decided to pull out all the stops in his attempt to remake Cathoon Castle in his image. He assembled the most talented builders, painters, gardeners, and artisans from all of the nearby villages and told them what he wanted them to do.

First and foremost, he wanted to see color. All that time he had spent with the Witch in her dank forest cavern had nearly driven him insane. Now he was going to take these gray castle walls and lighten them up. That meant warm colors, such as yellows and oranges, and cool ones, such as light blues and purples too, all swirling around on fields of white. Since it was now "his castle," he thought nothing wrong with any of the major changes he planned to make.

He hired the most talented glass masters to replace the windows in the great hall with stained glass ones depicting scenes of his "heroic escape" from the forest. There was nothing Caterwaul loved more than to lie on the floor while the sun shone through the windows and onto him. He assumed that having stained glass windows of varied colors would vary the temperature of the rays, and he was right. He especially liked to lie in the sun first thing in the morning. Sometimes he would remain there for hours unmoved. Then he'd stretch a bit and shift positions to allow exposure of every part of his fur to the warmth of the sun.

The outside of the castle grounds, he had manicured meticulously, and a hedgerow was planted in the form of a maze so that he could get his exercise for the day. He had ramps built, too, so he could run up and down on them, giving him hours and hours of enjoyment. Since he was a cat, he had special catwalks built to his design that spanned the castle both inside and out.

He replaced the old crystal chandeliers with imported mobiles, which almost always showed depictions of cats from faraway lands. He hoped someday to be able to travel to those places. Some of them made music when the wind blew across them like chimes. Caterwaul loved these best.

He had giant bird feeders constructed so he could gaze out the window and watch birds. *After all, who doesn't like to stare at birds?* he thought. He installed scratching posts in every room of the castle and filled them all with hundreds of cat toys. There was no doubt who was master of the castle now.

Last, he created an exercise room complete with balance beams, rings, and all sorts of gymnastic equipment. If there was going to be a whole slew of visitors, Caterwaul wanted to be sure they could keep themselves in decent shape.

The humans working at the castle all knew Caterwaul was in charge and they did whatever he asked of them. Caterwaul got along well with humans. However, out of the entire castle staff, the one Caterwaul liked most was Orris the chef. He considered Orris to be a friend, and he believed the feeling was mutual.

Orris often would sit at the koi pond beside his new master, who punched and prodded at the waters. He watched as the black cat swiped at the fish the way a boxer throws out his jab, and every now and then, Caterwaul would hook one of them on his claws.

If and when this happened, the cat would give the fish to Orris to prepare for an elaborate dinner. It might not be the same as one of the former queen's feasts, but still it gave Orris the practice he needed. However, this was something that did not happen often. Caterwaul, unlike most felines, liked to practice catch-and-release.

With every passing day, the castle became more Caterwaul's creation. He wondered what the queen would have to say if she saw it, then he briefly paused a moment to silently reflect upon his companion.

Caterwaul thought about what might have happened to Druciah. He missed her terribly. She had been good to him. The thought that she and her entourage might have been killed and eaten by a giant turtle disturbed him. But he was confident that if she were still alive, he certainly would have heard something by now.

7

To the Hollow Oak

After resting a few hours to regain strength, the party followed the possums' directions until it happened upon an enormous oak that was hollowed out with a huge door on it. The sun was just coming up over the canopy, and the queen and her entourage could see they had entered an unnatural place. Here the forest looked as if someone or something had spent a great deal of time carefully managing the surroundings. With the sun high in the sky, one could see the area around the hollowed-out tree was full of brilliant flowers and bushes, carefully arranged as if done by a professional gardener. The landscape was breathtaking, to say the least.

Remembering the prime minister's warning, the queen and her followers tried to slip by it, making very little noise. But they were in a forest, and because of this, no matter how they tried, they were doomed to dislodge something. Suddenly there was a snapping sound. Warwick Vane Bezel III accidentally stepped on a rather large twig, breaking it like a pretzel stick.

Suddenly the giant door swung open, and a large, enraged turtle leaped at them from the inside of the tree. The turtle was enormous. It was about as long as a man, or longer, with a head which must have been two feet wide at the least.

As he roared angrily, the queen noted he had a very attractive and multi-colored woolen scarf flowing over his shell and claws, which were carefully manicured and polished to a brilliant shine. His beak sparkled in the light, and he was wearing what appeared to be glitter all over his reptilian face. Then, of course, there was the eye makeup.

"Don't any of you touch anything! I have everything just the way I want it!" the turtle shouted at them with a most pronounced lisp. "I need you to just turn around right now, and go back the way you came, or I ssswear, I will sssnap you in half."

At this point, the queen, who had been somewhat prepared by Caterwaul for this inevitable encounter, stepped forward. "We apologize if we disturbed, you my good sir. We were sent this way by the Parliament of Possums. As soon as we came near it, we knew this place was obviously the home of a truly cultured soul. Let me again say how sorry we all are if we have disrupted things in any way."

The irritable turtle replied, "I find it hard to believe those dreadful possums with no sssense of ssstyle whatsoever would sssend anyone this way, especially when they know that upsetting Joffrey is the worst thing you can possibly do." The guards looked at each other with bewilderment as if to ask, *who is Joffrey?*

"Hello . . . that's ME . . . I'm Joffrey . . . you imbeciles!" said the turtle, anticipating exactly what they were thinking. "It took me years to get everything in this clearing just the way I want it. You can sssee all the work that went into this area around you, can't you?

"The possums know I don't like uninvited guests. Uninvited guests mess with MY things, and it's known far and wide throughout the forest that only people with a death wish ever mess with my things."

"Again, forgive us, Joffrey. I am Druciah, queen of the land from the edge of this forest to the sea. I seek an audience with the Witch of Red Moon Forest. I do not wish to disturb your beautiful and sophisticated decor. You obviously possess a flair for design second to none in these parts. Tell me friend, have you studied?"

The glitter on the turtle's face simulated blushing. "Why no," he said, "I learned to do this entirely on my own. There aren't many interior design classes open to turtles."

The queen continued her flattery. "Well, I love what you have done to the place, Joffrey. It's positively yummy. The color schemes are wonderful. They reveal a natural beauty unmatched by any royal decorator I have. If you didn't live all the way out here, I would employ you at the palace," the queen said with what appeared to be genuine adoration.

"Do you really think ssso? How kind of you to sssay. Obviously you have an eye for design at least as ssseasoned as my own."

By now any hint of hostility was gone from the turtle, and Joffrey invited the queen to enter his hollowed-out oak tree. "Your majesty, it just so happens that I have a pot of tea on the fire right now, and I would love it if you would join me. We can discuss what it is that you like most about what I have accomplished here. You do realize that I've had very little to work with."

Despite Warwick Vane Bezel III's misgivings, the queen accompanied Joffrey into the hollowed-out oak, emerging into a beautiful and cozy great room. She noticed his incredible attention to detail. The room was filled with fine tapestries and colorful window treatments. The hand-carved furniture was brilliant—which is especially impressive considering the hands that had carved the furniture belonged to a giant snapping turtle.

Joffrey brought the queen some tea.

She took a sip and acknowledged its quality. "I have a gift for you Joffrey that I think you are going to absolutely love."

The queen walked to the great door and called out, "Guards, bring me the cedar chest!"

Once it had been moved inside the oak tree, the queen opened the chest to reveal two pairs of hand-stitched throw pillows decorated with intricate gold embroidery. The chest also contained some very fine draperies and an array of decorative knick-knacks fit for only the wealthiest households. Also included was a set of the finest bed linens and a down comforter fit for a royal bedchamber. Last, she unrolled a small but intricate hand-woven rug and set it by the front door.

"Well what do you think?" asked the queen. "If there is anything you find you don't like, you can always give it to the possums. They did make our meeting today possible after all."

Joffrey fell to what Druciah assumed were his knees, but one can never tell with turtles. "Why your majesty, these gifts are sssimply exquisite. What a truly fabulous present this is. Every sssingle item is absolutely gorgeous. You truly have the eye, my queen." The turtle was grinning and clapping his front turtle paws together. He had never in his life been given such a present as this chest full of goods.

"Nobody has ever given me anything like this. And to think, I almost bit you and your sssilly henchmen in half." He was ashamed. "Can you ever forgive me, my queen? You are welcome here anytime. Do you like show tunes?"

It was the happiest day of Joffrey's reptilian life. "You sssay you are going to sssee the Witch? Is there anything I can do to make you change your mind? She's not much fun, and ssshe has a really awful sssense of personal hygiene.

"And that cave ssshe lives in . . . well, let's just come out and sssay it: IT'S A CAVE! Really, all that magic at her disposal, and ssshe chooses to live in that filthy dirty cave of all places . . . and her personal appearance? Not exactly haute couture, if you'll pardon my French! If I were her, the first thing I'd do would be to conjure up sssome high heels and lots and lots of makeup . . . oh, and a corset to hide that unsightly figure of hers.

"Maybe get sssome colorful new clothes. You know they sssay that black is ssslimming, but that wardrobe of hers is ssso depressing . . . I tell you what ssshe really needs is a complete makeover, but please don't tell her I sssaid that. That would be hateful."

Joffrey rambled on. "Are you really sssure you want to visit her of all people? Why don't you just ssstay here tonight? We can order take-out. It will be fun. Do you guys like fish?" He clapped his massive paws together as he suggested this.

"As tempting as your offer is, I must decline. I have pressing personal matters I must discuss with the Witch and as much as it pains me to leave you, I am afraid I must. If we may but pass, I promise that I will call on you to be my guest at the palace in the near future," said Druciah.

"Oh that would be lovely," said Joffrey, "and maybe then we could talk sssome more about that job." The turtle gathered up the dishes and made sure to wipe down any surfaces that either he or Druciah might have touched. He smiled at the queen, embarrassed. "OCD, that's me," he giggled sporting his enormous snapping turtle grin.

Once they had gone back outside, the turtle addressed the entire party. "Well if you insist on going, I feel compelled to warn you about those irritating frogs at Bug SSStool Creek. They ssstand guard over the path for the Witch. They don't really do it out of choice, mind you, but they are cursed. They really don't like her at all.

"Now for sssomeone like me, the frogs don't present much of a problem." He tapped his armored shell, "Natural body armor and all that." He continued, "For me they are just a pain in my ssstubby tail, but for you they could be quite dangerous.

"They have these wish bones which they use as makeshift

bows and filed-down porcupine quills which they use as arrows. They dip the arrows in the poisons on their back, and then they fire at any trespassers. You guys are going to need sssomething to protect you from those sssilly little darts. Luckily, I think I may just have the thing to help. Wait here . . . I'll be right back."

Joffrey went back into his tree, and after a few minutes, he returned holding five really elaborate suits of fish mail. "Contrary to popular belief, I do have friends. Granted I can count them on two paws," he was laughing. "But when Carlos and his friends come to visit they insist on gathering crawfish. They like to make étouffée from those ssslimy little creek insects. So, for protection, I ssstitched together sssome wonderful outerwear from fish ssscales woven together with Ssspanish moss to create a kind of ssstylish, lightweight armor.

"It won't help you in a real fight, mind you, but it ssseems to repel those annoying darts. I can let you borrow them if you promise me you'll bring them back," said the turtle. He passed them around to the queen and her group, making sure that the queen got the prettiest and Warwick Vane Bezel III, the clunkiest. "Hopefully this one will fit you, big boy," he said to the commander, winking.

"How truly gracious of you, Joffrey," the queen said. "Words cannot begin to express my thanks." They all put on Joffrey's creations. "You know I haven't had this much fun in years. I really need to get out of the castle more often. Your generosity will be remembered."

After they all had time to put on the armor, Joffrey smiled. They looked very slick in his creations.

"Your majesty, you look marvelous, if I do sssay so myself. Ssstylish but functional: that's my motto. These outfits ssshould protect you, but try not to get them too dirty. Have you any idea how hard it is to get ssstains out of Ssspanish moss?" Joffrey minced.

Then something else occurred to the turtle. "Ooh . . . just hold those positions. You all look ssso good, especially you, my handsome friend. Absolutely dashing!" He winked again at Warwick, who shifted uncomfortably. "Ssstay there . . . all of you. I will be right back."

This time Joffrey went inside the oak and returned with a mirror. "You guys just have to see how fabulous you all look."

The queen, Warwick, and two of the guards turned their heads quickly away and shut their eyes. "No Joffrey, no mirrors please!" she shouted. Unfortunately for the queen, the third guard was more fashion-conscious than the others. He sucked in his gut and posed, looking straight into the mirror. Poof, he disappeared and in his place was a long-haired Persian cat, who upon seeing a large and hungry-looking snapping turtle, scampered quickly away into the woods.

"Well," said Joffrey astonished, "I have to sssay that that has never happened before. I wonder what could have caused that?"

"I have no earthly idea," the queen lied. "But whatever it is, it has to be supernatural. That's why we need to see the Witch so badly. All I know is that people all over my kingdom are turning into cats, and mirrors are involved. If anyone has the answer, we believe it is the Witch."

"You may be right, your majesty. The Witch used to have a cat. It was a big, bushy, black one. But then one day, it just disappeared on her. When she found out that he was missing, she was terribly upset. Do you think that she put a curse on mirrors as a way to mourn the loss of her pet?" he inquired. "I know that she loved him very much."

"It may just be, Joffrey," said Druciah. "That's what we are hoping to find out."

It was amazing how easy it was for the queen to slip right back into her evil self. For a while it seemed that her journey had changed her, and perhaps it had, briefly. But even if her encounters with the Parliament of Possums and Joffrey the designing turtle had brought some fun into her life, it was only temporary and not enough to erase the years of hatred and jealousy that had reshaped her soul in darkness.

She was motivated again to soldier on. She had a mission and that was to find the Witch of Red Moon Forest,

8

The Poison Dart Frogs of Bug Stool Creek

"This is all going according to plan, Warwick," said the queen as the group, now one guard short, moved on down the path. The forest seemed to Druciah to be sentient, like it was watching them carefully as they descended deeper into the thickness of the wood. As they pressed on, they could feel its eyes all around them.

The air was thick with humidity, and they all grew tense. As they approached the creek bed, they heard a tiny voice shout, "FIRE!"

All of a sudden, a barrage of tiny arrows came from all directions. It was a full-fledged ambush that went on for several minutes. The darts bounced off of their fish-scale clothing just as Joffrey said it would. Not a single quill penetrated the armor.

"Praise our reptilian friend, my suit is repelling every shot," said one of the guards.

"Cease fire!" said the tiny voice. "Did you say reptilian friend?" Warwick Vane Bezel III turned his head all around, looking for the source of the orders. "Joffrey's been at it again boys!" the voice screamed. Just then hundreds of frogs appeared, climbing down the Spanish moss, gathering in ranks, military-style. They were brightly colored with glossy black patterns that resembled camouflage. Most of them were yellow or yellow-green, but there was the occasional red or blue one in their midst. The largest among them could not have been more than three inches in length.

The frog, who appeared to be the leader, hopped forward. Warwick Vane Bezel III resisted the urge to squash him with his boot.

"I am General Fairfax, leader of the Poison Dart Frogs of Bug Stool Creek, and you are trespassing. You have no right to be here." The general was one of the larger of the frogs. He was yellowish green and black and wore a tiny tailored officer's jacket complete with a red sash and gold epaulettes. On his head he wore an equally tiny black Marshals hat with fur trimmings. "Retreat now and we will not subject you to our curse," he said with authority.

"Your curse?" the queen inquired. "Tell me, my tiny general, how are you cursed?"

"Once we were men," said Fairfax, before letting out a loud *ribbit*. "The Witch cursed us. Now we guard this creek. It is our sole purpose. I will tell you again that you must turn back, or we will fire. There are hundreds of us, and we all are armed. If even one of our poison arrows pierces your skin, you will change into a frog like us."

Warwick Vane Bezel III looked at Fairfax incredulously, but the general continued. "My frogs are excellent marksmen, and I can promise you they will find the holes in that fish-scale clothing that no-good turtle gave you."

The queen was only half-listening. Something the frog said had her thinking. "Fairfax?" she said, "I remember a General Fairfax from years ago, when I was a small child. Are you the Fairfax who was the leader of my father's army?"

"I was a general in Harsizzle's army long ago." He paused and then quietly queried, "You are little Druciah?"

"Not little anymore," she answered. "I have ruled in Harsizzle for more than twenty years, since my father's unfortunate and untimely passing. What happened to you, General? We all assumed that you were dead."

"Have I been here for that long?" the frog asked, not expecting an answer. "The king . . . dead? More than twenty years, you say?"

"Yes, General," the queen answered. "It has been a long time. But focus now and tell me what happened."

"Yes . . . yes," he said slowly as if shaking the cobwebs from his memory. "Your father sent me to council with the Witch because he was fearful of an uprising among the Folland people to our north. Though they had been quiet for generations, there were rumors of a famine in their country, which your father thought might cause the nomads to migrate south.

"Your father thought he could gain some advantage by making a covenant with the woodland sorceress. So I and ten of my men chopped through the thick trees for many days until we finally reached this place they call Bug Stool Creek." There was sadness in his voice.

"Nobody told us the forest had certain 'rules' that had to be followed. We began our hacking and slashing in broad daylight. The wood seemed to fight us. If we had only waited until nightfall, things might have gone differently. Not one of us had the slightest idea we were being watched . . . and judged by her.

"It was only after we arrived at this stream that my fate, and that of my men, was sealed. I took a tiny arrow to the cheek. All ten of my men were hit by poison darts. I saw them topple as I felt the consciousness drain from me. When I awoke, I was in this form as you see me now. As you can see, our numbers have grown over time." He rubbed at his tiny frog moustache.

"I warn you again, Queen Druciah, out of the great respect and love I had for your father, leave this forest now, for in this froggy form, we have no control of ourselves. We are but slaves. We live only to serve the Witch."

"How positively awful, General," said the queen, feigning concern. "Surely there must be some way that you can break this hold that the Witch has over you?"

Just then, one of the frogs saw an opening. One of the two remaining guards had an itch on his left flank and instinctively moved his hand there to scratch it. As he dragged his nails over the irritated spot, he accidentally raised the fish-scale shirt Joffrey had given him. There was now easily an inch of bare skin unprotected. The frog fired his poisoned porcupine quill, and it lodged itself in the guard's exposed buttocks.

The guard leaped into the air, and before his feet could reconnect with earth, he was transformed into a frog. The fish-scale outfit remained, however, and it dropped into the muck of the creek bank. The former guard hopped clumsily across the creek and joined the other frogs in one of the back ranks. Warwick Vane Bezel III grabbed up the garment and put it in his pack.

"General, please, in the name of my father, the king, please do not fire on us again!" implored the queen.

"I'm sorry, your majesty, for I gave no order to fire." Fairfax was enraged that one of his soldiers would act without orders. After all, if you don't have discipline in an army, what do you have?

"Listen up, you treacherous tadpoles!" he growled. His throat pouch was trembling with the air he was taking in. He was a frog who was used to being obeyed. "If any more shots are fired at the queen or her companions, I am going to deep-fry the shooter's legs and serve them up to those pitiable possums. Am I understood?

"And as for the amphibious anarchist who fired that last shot without my command, I want you to give me fifty pushups, froggy-style." He looked straight at the shooter. "That means front legs only, now! Somebody count 'em off!" the General shouted.

Fairfax returned his attention to Druciah. "I believe you're safe now, your majesty. You should turn around and get out of here while you still have time. This is no place for royalty, this cesspool of darkness. Save yourself," pleaded the frog.

"I appreciate your warnings, General, but I must press on. I have to find that Witch," the queen insisted.

"Well if you must go, follow the flow of the creek for about half a kilometer, and you will find what you are looking for. But don't say I didn't warn you, your highness. Witches aren't the best sorts of people. I don't expect I will see you again."

General Fairfax kicked his rear legs together and raised a webbed foot to his forehead in a salute, and then he and the other frogs disappeared into the cover.

The queen, Warwick Vane Bezel III, and the last of her guards followed the creek bed for half a kilometer as directed by Fairfax, sidestepping slippery rocks and the occasional water snake. It occurred to her that every step they took might just bring them a step closer to their doom. She imagined she could hear her companions' heartbeats. They sounded like arrhythmic drums beating uncontrollably. They were now in the darkest part of the forest. The smells of decaying plants and termite-infested tree trunks were palatable. Then as if at once, all of the natural sounds of the forest went silent. They had arrived at the cave of the Witch.

Druciah could tell it was an ancient cave, carved out eons ago by the blood of some long-extinct volcano. Warwick Vane

Bezel III pointed to an old sign above the cave and said, "Look here, it has ancient writing on it." On closer inspection, it happened that the words were not ancient at all, but read "KEEP OUT! THAT MEANS YE!"

Suddenly a voice seemed to come from nowhere and said "Hold there; you're the queen aren't you? You don't want to go in there."

"Where are you, and why can't I see you?" asked the queen.

"I'm down 'ere," said the voice. "Or what's left of me, that is." Druciah looked down to see a large and slender rat. He was laughing and smiling with big yellow teeth. In front of him was the core of some long-rotten piece of fruit, and he took the occasional gnaw at it.

"My name's Edsel. I used to be a blacksmith in Harsizzle, but I couldn't afford to pay your taxes . . . so I asked this nice old woman in the village if I could borrow some coin. Now, my business didn't pick up and I couldn't pay her back. Didn't really think it was that big of a deal. I meant to. But anyway as it turns out, the old woman had a sister. You'll never guess who.

"So one night I'm sitting 'round, minding my own business having a bit o' cheese, and there is a knock on me door. I open it and there is this other old woman standing there all in black—not slimming at all, if you ask me. I think she coulda benefitted from some high heels and a bit of makeup, not to get off the point . . . but she starts telling me that I need to pay her sister back the money I owes her.

"So I says to her. 'Hey, what's all this then? Fancy a bit of cheese?' I mean a woman is a woman, if ya know what I mean." He winked and leaned against a nearby rock. "So I tells her I don't have the money and ask her what she's gonna do about it? And she turned me into a rat."

By now Druciah felt that she had stumbled into something

truly awful. Here was a rat that loved to hear himself talk.

The rat kept rolling, "So that's how I became this handsome fellow you see before you now. Don't care all that much really. It's quite a wonderful coat she gave me, don't you think?" He looked at himself. "Bit greasy maybe.

"Every thing's all right though, 'cept for the snakes . . . I don't like them much at all. Always trying to trick me into becoming their dinner," he paused long enough to catch his breath.

"I never thought in a million years I would be staring at your face. Of all people in all the possible places, Queen Druciah! Ha, who would have imagined? There were several times I reckoned as to what I might say to you if I had the chance. But now, everything escapes me. This is just brilliant. You and me, together, here in the mouth of this filthy cave, just brilliant.

"And who is that with you? Who else but Warwick Vane Bezel III? Amazing . . . Hello, constable. Shouldn't you be back in Harsizzle plundering, stealing, and causing grievous bodily harm? It is Friday night, you know. I remember just a few years back how you busted down me door, walked right over to the pot of stew I had on the fire and just took it. I had been working on that stew for hours. Then you bashed me over the head with your cudgel and left me there bleeding . . . you bloody Neanderthal. You two are just right for each other. A couple of heartless animals you are," he rambled.

The queen stood there aghast, her mouth hanging open. She could not believe what she was hearing from this insolent rodent. He simply would not shut up.

"And another thing . . . How did you expect for me to pay more in taxes than I made? I gotta eat, too. You're not too good at the mathematics are you? You left me destitute while you used my tax dollars to throw all those extravagant parties. Parties I wasn't even invited to. I'm almost glad I am here now so I don't have to hear your name or anguish about big boy here come crashing through me door. I am happy as a rat because that's all I ever was as a human. At least now, I don't have to be pretentious."

"Well, Edsel," interjected the queen, hoping to get a chance to speak before the rat resumed his ranting. "If you will give me a moment to retort, I will attempt to do so.

"I've . . . uh . . . recently discovered that there has been a spell on me for many years, and I have finally concluded that the Witch is responsible." The queen was scrambling to come up with a story quickly. This was not a position she often found herself in. "That is me, all my guards and taxmen, and Warwick Vane Bezel III too. I have traveled here at great expense and endured this wretched forest to see if . . . uh . . . I could get the spell lifted so that I can right all the wrongs that have been committed in my name. Now don't you appreciate my sacrifices?"

"Tell it to someone else, Queenie. You don't expect me to believe that, do you? I may be a rat, but please don't assume that I am daft. The Witch put a spell on you? Tell me some more porky pies. You're not pulling any wool over these eyes, I tell you. That's rich . . . Like somehow it was the Witch who made you the greedy thing that you are. I tell you this. You don't need help being rotten. You practically invented it."

She was dumbfounded.

"Just go on down . . . you know she's waiting for you. She's got eyes everywhere, she has. She's known you're coming ever since you set foot in Red Moon." He gestured that she should follow the path as it went deep into the cave.

With their every step, it got darker. Warwick lit a torch, but even by the torchlight the cave seemed to go on and on. It was the smells they noticed first. They were initially faint, but gained in intensity as they moved along the path.

First, there was a really foul and pungent smell like a stagnant water pool. The walls of the cave were bleeding moisture, and Druciah guessed they must be near an underground stream. Next, the scent was joined by a smell of rotting wood. Tree roots stuck through the wet clay walls in a massive tangle. Some of them were rotten as if they supported trees on the surface that had long ago died off. Mushrooms and other fungi feasted on the decaying wood.

Warwick Vane Bezel III noticed that there seemed to be no animals about. It was unusual, he thought. In fact, he couldn't recall seeing even an insect since they'd left Edsel. Soon they came to notice the signs of habitation. The mud walls were gone and the party found itself surrounded by clean, bare rock. Notches carved out of the walls housed small glass jars, each of which emitted a strange green light. Warwick nodded to the guard to examine one.

The glow was generated by the bodies of luminescent caterpillars gingerly feasting on vine leaves. It really was ingenious. It was a natural adaptation of insect larvae that the Witch had adopted for her purposes. The cave path was now actually well lit, and the party soon came to a door, which was slightly ajar. The queen pushed it slightly, and it opened, revealing a good-sized room. There was a woven grass mat just inside the door, upon which was written the word "Welcome."

"Wipe your feet," called a voice from within the room.

The room was lit by torches and candles that flickered in a smoky haze. Still, even squinting, it was difficult to see inside.

"Wipe your feet," said the voice again. "What, were you raised in a barn? There's a mat there for a reason. Your feet are filthy. I don't like it when people track mud into my home."

It was difficult to see far into the room, but as they moved further inside, the queen was able to make out the shape of a woman. She was dressed all in black and had long, matted, gray hair. She was sitting on a rickety, old chair. The queen and her party moved deeper into the room, first carefully cleaning the dirt from their shoes.

"Is there a chance that any of you lot plays chess?" she asked.

Knight Takes Pawn

hess," the Witch repeated. "You look like civilized folks, surely you know the game? I would like to play."

"I play," answered Druciah.

"Are you any good?" the Witch inquired, tilting her head to the side the way a parrot might. The torchlight emphasized the opaque whiteness of her cataract. "I haven't had a game of chess in a while, but it's been longer still since I played anyone worth his salt." The Witch rose from her seat and walked over to a shelf and grabbed a wooden box. "Come over here and sit by me. Your men too; tell them to make themselves comfortable."

There were few places to sit, and none of them looked particularly comfortable. Still Warwick Vane Bezel III and the guard sat down.

"My playing partners have been limited of late and no challenge either. The rat can't play at all, I'm afraid. You and I shall have a game, Druciah," the Witch said.

The queen moved a rickety chair over to a table and the Witch moved her chair accordingly. She opened the wooden box and revealed an intricately carved set of chess pieces. The carvings were beautiful, the work of a master.

"This game set was given to me long ago by my grandfather,"

she said as she began to set the pieces. "I always play black, my dear, so you will go first."

Druciah picked up the white queen. She gently rubbed her index figure over its contours. "Beautiful," she whispered. It was the most detailed chess piece she had ever seen. She put the piece down on its appropriate square. "How do you know my name?" she asked.

The Witch chuckled. "I know lots of things. Some of them not so pleasant and I would prefer not to remember them." She finished setting the pieces. "My dear, there is nothing that goes on in my forest that I am not aware of." She smiled slyly. A few of her teeth were no longer there.

"A game then?" she said. "It's your move, white."

Druciah moved her queen's pawn forward two spaces.

The Witch grinned. "Interesting. You may give me a game after all. You are either very bold or very stupid. We shall see which one it is." She countered with her own queen's pawn cutting off Druciah's.

White followed by moving her left-hand knight in front of her bishop's pawn. Black countered by moving her right-hand bishop's pawn up two spaces.

Druciah next moved her knight to take the Witch's queen's pawn.

"Aha!" said the Witch. "You are a player." She took her finger and knocked over her own queen indicating her concession.

"Why did you do that? We'd only just begun playing," asked the queen.

"I can see very clearly that you have me, my dear. In twelve moves, most likely. You are a very clever player. Not everybody would have the audacity to play a counter-gambit like that with white."

The Witch picked up the pieces and returned them to the

box. "Tell me why you are here, my love. I am open to some arrangement. But know this before we go any further. One of the things that I am going to demand of you is the return of my cat."

"Your cat?" asked the queen. She was about to lie to the Witch, then thought better on it.

"I suspected that you might have him, and your chess opening betrays you. The opening moves you made are from what we chess aficionados call the Keravian Gambit. It is a bold strategy indeed, and not one that I would expect from anyone but the best of players. It is a strategy used often by my cat. He once beat me in eleven moves with that advance.

"Logic tells me that you have played against my former pet and he has beaten you with that angle. You observed his play and now you use it against me. Clever, but I expected it. You are exposed. He must have told you about me and my powers. So tell me, why have you come here?"

By now Druciah's eyes had adjusted to the lights and smoke. She looked around. The Witch's cavern did not look so ominous. It hardly looked "witchy" at all. It's true that there were books. In fact, there were lots and lots of books, and scrolls, and stacks of papers and parchments. But it did not look like the majority of them were magic tomes. In fact, the cavern was overstuffed with all sorts of things that Druciah could only call junk.

There was a wall filled with jars and bottles, which the queen assumed were magical in nature, but right next to that was a counter heaped with the crockery and leftover remains of several meals. The cauldron on the fire seemed to have some kind of vegetable stew cooking in it. This place hardly seemed like the home of a sorceress.

On closer inspection, the old woman hardly looked like a witch at all. In fact Warwick Vane Bezel III thought she appeared more like a sad old woman. Like the kind of sad woman who lived a very lonely life underground, here in this dark cave miles away from anybody else. She could have been anyone's grandmother, if that anyone was the kind to abandon her grandmother to fend for herself here in Red Moon Forest.

The Witch spoke again, "My cat was my only real companion, but this cave was no home for an animal like him. He needed to roam, to explore, and to see more of the world around him. That is why, as much as it pained me to do so, I let him go."

The queen looked surprised.

"You find this hard to believe, Druciah? That I let my Caterwaul go away from me? Why? He is my only friend. I love him, and I could not bear to see him feeling like a prisoner. So I let him go . . . and now I am miserable."

The queen smiled. She now felt that in this new game, she had the upper hand. "Well then, I will not dance about the bush," Druciah said gliding around the room. "You know who I am, no doubt. As it happens, we can help each other. I have something you want, and you possess something I need. Though he appeared to me as a stray, the cat is no doubt yours, so I will return him to you.

"He won't come willingly, so you will have to prepare for me some type of sedative which I can place in his food. In exchange I need from you only a small thing. In return for your pet, you will consult your catalogue of spells and give me back my youth. I want to be young and beautiful for nine lifetimes."

She went on, "I want to be as I was years ago, blossoming and beautiful as an apple tree in spring. I want to rule unblemished by time for nine lifetimes. I want to be as fair as the summer flowers and as timeless as the sea. Can you do this for me?" Druciah asked.

"Of course I can, my vain queen," the Witch grinned. "But let me warn you. If you try to lie or cheat and do not return

Caterwaul to me, I will come after you, and I assure you that you will not like it if I do.

"So are we then agreed?" asked the Witch.

"Agreed," said Druciah happily.

"Well, now that this is settled, we have work to do," the Witch said as she slid a ladder around the room. She climbed nimbly up to the top right corner of a bookshelf and retrieved an ancient, dog-eared manuscript. Its pages were yellow and stained, and it had no cover. Climbing down, she walked over to the fireplace for more light. Flipping through the pages, she began to smile. "Ah . . . here it is. This is one of the oldest and most dangerous spells I have ever known." She giggled. "It is a recipe for a pie."

The queen looked at her confused. "Did I understand you correctly? Did you say pie?" Druciah inquired. The Witch blew the dust off the pages into the fire, causing the dust particles to burn like tiny fireflies.

"Yes, my dear, your hearing is perfectly fine. I did say pie. What I have here is the recipe for creating an ancient confection of deliciousness guaranteed to make you young again and for the requisite nine lifetimes. It is the recipe for *feline pie*," the Witch said with a snicker.

"It requires some preparation, so you will need someone who understands his way around the kitchen. Judging from how spoiled you appear to be, I am sure that you have someone you can trust to make it for you.

"The ingredients must be gathered with great care and followed explicitly according to my instructions. You may find some of the more unconventional ingredients in the forest on your way back. The rest can be assembled with what's already in your kitchen, I'd imagine." The Witch paused for a minute reading the fundamentals of the dessert. She handed Druciah a piece of paper and some charcoal and began to dictate the recipe.

"Begin the pie with whatever pie dough recipe you like. I prefer to add in some white sugar and honey. This will give you a mild and buttery taste. You can substitute brown sugar for the honey if you don't feel like getting stung," she giggled. "But doing so will give the pie more of a caramel flavor. I don't particularly care for caramel myself, but each according to her taste.

"Prepare a nine-inch pie pan; it's best if you use a glass one, my dear. Place the crust in it evenly and glaze it with the yolks of at least two eggs. You need to have the temperature of your oven preheated to about 375 degrees while you gather a bowl to mix the filling."

Her voice became suddenly more "witch-like" as she recited to Druciah the components for the pie's filling.

"*1 cup of sugar, 4 large eggs, 6 tablespoons of unsalted butter—you have to use unsalted butter, no exception—2 tablespoons of vanilla, 1/4 cup of dark rum, one eye of salamander, 2 owl beaks, six leaves of the althea plant, threads from the golden seal root, a pinch of feverfew, the pinky toe of a rat, the slime of an immature toad, a pinch of salt, and the tail of a white female cat.*"

The Witch paused to see if Druciah had gotten it all down correctly. "Now you must combine the ingredients, all except the cat's tail, together in a large bowl while warming the crust until hot. Place the cat's tail in the pie pan, pour the filling on top of it and cover with a rolled out top crust."

The queen shook her hand to keep it from cramping.

"Poke some holes in the top so the steam can escape and brush the top of the pie with more of the egg yolk to ensure that it bakes to a golden brown." The Witch hungrily smacked her lips together. "Make sure you bake it for between forty-five and fifty minutes; remember some ovens are hotter than others. You will want to take it out once the top is golden brown. Let it stand for one hour before eating," the Witch finished.

"Is that everything?" Druciah asked exhaustedly. "I will have Orris, my chef, attend to its creation when I return. He is unmatched in the preparation of palatable pleasures." The queen paused for a second, admiring her alliteration, and then asked, "Now, how am I going to catch Caterwaul for you? He is a tricky ball of fur. All my guards could not catch him if their lives depended on it."

The Witch walked over to where several potions crowded the top of a tiny table. She picked up several one by one, removing the tops and sniffing each until she found what she was looking for.

"Here . . . this will do the trick," she said to the queen. "Place three drops of this in his food, and it should knock him out long enough for you to complete your journey from the castle to here. It won't hurt him; it will simply put him out for the duration of your trip." She paused, and then said hopefully, "I will be so happy to have him back. He is the only real friend I have."

The Witch poured a small amount of the elixir into a small, green-glass phial.

"I suppose you find it easy to let him go?" the Witch continued. "That proves to me you could never love another. Tell me, queen, when your wish is granted, who will you call friend? You have one, and yet you betray him. I suspect that I will soon have one more friend than you, your highness."

The queen sneered at what she saw as a challenge. "I will be loved again by many," she said. "You don't know what you are talking about, hag. Cathoon Castle will soon be filled with laughter. It will shake once again with grand parties and succulent feasts. I shall be beautiful again and for ages." She spat on the ground. "I will return with your chess partner as soon as I can."

The queen turned and exited defiantly up the corridor, followed by her last remaining guard. However, Warwick Vane Bezel III, chief constable of the queen's secret police force, stayed behind for a moment. Scratching his head in wonder, he looked at the Witch and asked, "Can I have a bite of what you're cooking? It smells great."

10

A Whole New Paint Job

On her way out of the forest, Druciah made sure to stop by to say farewell to General Fairfax. She vowed to do whatever she could to release him from the Witch's curse, but until then, she wished him the best.

The general had been honestly glad to see her. Though he had been surprised to learn just how long he had been trapped as a frog, he remembered her as an innocent and wide-eyed girl and thus knew nothing of her true character. Shouting "about face," to the other frogs, they turned as one before hopping off into the forest.

Joffrey was not so happy to see them, at least at first. He was a bit perturbed that one of his outfits came back to him covered in the muck of the forest floor. However, after the queen explained that the guard who was wearing it was now a frog, he couldn't really stay too upset.

Druciah again reminded him that she would soon be inviting him to the castle. How she would explain the presence of a man-sized snapping turtle, who was also an interior designer, was something she'd worry about later.

Approaching the possums' clearing, the queen was happy to find the Parliament was too involved in secret negotiations with the Assembly of Animals to be disturbed. As the party approached their domains, they saw signs that read, "No humans allowed."

She was glad of this because she did not want to have to stop for more pleasantries. She was anxious to get back to Cathoon Castle.

After a while, the queen and her remaining escorts emerged from the forest. Druciah cleaned herself up and climbed up into her coach. She sent her guard and Warwick Vane Bezel III back into the woods to secure those ingredients she knew were sure to be absent from Orris's pantry. After about an hour, when they returned, Warwick was covered in filth.

"What in the world happened to you?" the queen asked.

"I fell into the swamp trying to nab your bloody salamander," he said handing her a muddy bag. "I got them all though. Every single last disgusting item, just like you asked me to."

He wiped his muddy face clean on his sleeve.

~

As is usually the case on such journeys, the group made better time in going than in the coming. Druciah was conscious of the fact that they had been gone a long time. The coach driver, with the queen constantly in his ear, wanted to get back to the castle as soon as possible just to shut her up. The two extra horses helped out a lot in that regard.

Again the word got around that the queen and her secret policeman were on their way. As before, the people ran away and hid. There was almost no sign of life anywhere except for the occasional kitty that scurried across their path. They stopped several times to water the horses, helping themselves to any food that the townsfolk had left behind.

Often it appeared that the inhabitants had been cooking only moments before evacuating the premises. As Queen Druciah rode through the various villages and towns, she noticed the twinkling of light reflecting off the fragments of all the shattered mirrors broken along the way.

"There is no telling how many years of bad luck are lurking in that rubbish, Warwick!" the queen shouted to Vane Bezel jokingly. Warwick was riding his warhorse beside her coach. The queen laughed out loud. She was elated. Very soon she would have her youth and beauty back.

I mustn't forget to have Caterwaul release the spell, she thought to herself. I will have him do it just as soon as he brings me a solid-white, female cat. She smiled wickedly. His chances are better if we wait.

You can imagine Druciah's confusion when she saw what the cat had done to the landscape outside Cathoon as her coach rolled up to the castle. It was shocking to the queen to see her home turned into a feline paradise.

The queen stepped from her carriage and went directly inside in search of her mischievous pet. Going from room to room, her guard in tow, she found that the cat's alteration to the castle's interior was even worse than the exterior. She finally found him alone, sunbathing in the solarium asleep, awkwardly stretched out on his back across a large pillow. A bit of kitty drool dangled from his mouth. He was having a catnap and obviously dreaming.

"Caterwaul!" She shouted. "What have you done to my Cathoon? It looks like a . . . a . . . cat house!"

Caterwaul shot up at once. The bit of drool slapped him in his left eye and he began trembling as if he'd seen a ghost. After all, she had been gone for a very long time.

"Queen Druciah," he said in a trembling voice as if he'd seen a ghost, "I thought I would surprise you. Do you like it?"

It was all the queen could do to suppress her rage. "Well, I see you've been quite busy, my mischievous little friend." The queen sucked it up, trying not to give him any hint of his fate. "You know . . . Actually, I kind of like it," she said with sarcastic disgust.

She looked at him with deliberate intent. "What has transpired here in my absence is of little concern right now. We will talk about it later. The only thing that concerns me now is that I am back, and I have a job for you."

Feeling as though he had at least temporarily avoided her wrath, Caterwaul spoke. "I am happy to see you again, your majesty. If there is any part of the castle that displeases you, I will attend to it immediately," he said apologetically.

"We will leave it as is for now," said the queen. If she had harbored any doubts about giving him back to the Witch, they were all gone now.

"Did you get to see the Witch? What did she say? Did she give you what you were looking for?" His questions came hard and fast. He was confused by the fact that she still looked the same as she had when she left, although there may have been a few more errant hairs on her face.

"I need you to forget about all of that right now," she said. "Ask me no more questions. What I need you to do for me now is to go out among the villages and retrieve for me an all-white, female cat."

She drew extremely close to him to emphasize her point. "It is of the utmost importance that she be completely white with no stripes, spots, or speckles whatsoever. Is that clear? And you will have to be quick about it because I need her back here as soon as possible."

"Your majesty," Caterwaul answered, "that's a strange request. Of course I will go as soon as possible, but why do you need her?" Caterwaul asked.

"I said no questions. Bring me a white, female cat as I have requested. All will be revealed to you in time. Now do as I ask."

The cat stretched his limbs, stood at attention, and said, "Don't worry, my queen. I will bring you back the most beautiful cat in the kingdom."

~

Caterwaul gathered what he'd need for the trip. He stopped by to see Orris on his way out. The two had become good friends since the queen left. The chef prepared enough food to put in his cat-sized backpack for his travels. The remaining room in the pack he used to carry the magic powders and potions he could need to deal with problems that might arise along the way.

Orris had come to like having Caterwaul in charge of the castle. He had been enjoying life again. He was not happy now. With the return of the queen, his life at Cathoon was sure to go back to the way it was before. He wasn't looking forward to that at all.

The queen looked around the castle at what "damage" the cat had done. *As soon as he is returned to the Witch, I will do some renovating myself. I will create a new Cathoon worthy of an empress, she thought to herself. I will have all of these cat things removed from the premises and burned.*

Caterwaul will be erased from my memory. I will be young, and as such, I will have new young suitors to keep me occupied. Most importantly, I will be feared. She thought all of these things as she put the sack that Warwick Vane Bezel III had given her high on a shelf in the armoire in her bedchamber for safekeeping.

Part II

Heroes and Villains

11

To Harsizzle

Caterwaul strolled into the village of Harsizzle. "It's been so long since I've been just a cat, I don't know where to start," he muttered to himself. He'd lived most of his life with the Witch of Red Moon Forest, and she didn't often have visitors, much less of the cat variety. He roamed through the village streets, noticing all of the smells and sounds he remembered from back when he was just a small kitten.

Unsurprisingly, it seemed everywhere he glanced in town he saw cats. There were so very many of them. Wherever he went, there they were: in the windows, in the doorways, in the alleyways, and on the streets.

Many of them looked hungry and more than a bit scared. This was understandable since only a short while ago many of them had been humans. He noted that there were a number who were still just getting the hang of walking on all fours. Caterwaul sat for a while watching, as it was quite hilarious for a cat who had been one all his life to see all of these new ones trying to adjust.

In some houses, Caterwaul could hear the crying of the people who remained, wailing about what had happened to their husbands, wives, daughters, and sons. What sort of horrible creature could be responsible for this?

Surely it was sorcery . . . a truly monstrous deed. What had they done to deserve this awful fate? These were the questions on the lips of those who had not been changed. Caterwaul shook uncomfortably because he knew he was responsible. It was true he was following the queen's orders, but now he felt that he could have, and that perhaps he should have, said no. Curling up in a hole underneath one of the empty houses, he fell asleep.

Several hours later, he awoke to the sound of rain. It was coming down in buckets. Backing away from the opening to a safer position, he avoided the rush of water, which flowed, past his hideaway. He took the downpour as a good sign. From personal experience, he knew that cats do not like rainstorms, and he could hear the cries of his feline brethren as they dashed about looking for the nearest shelter. He thought that the cloudburst would make finding the white cat easy. All he needed to do was go to the places where the cats were hiding, waiting for the rain to pass.

The storm eased up long enough for Caterwaul to venture out. It was still more than a drizzle, but it was no longer the torrent it had been. Up ahead, he thought he saw a place likely to be full of refugees.

It was an old abandoned building that looked like it had at one time been used for some sort of local industry. He could hear the many catcalls as he approached. It sounded as if some of the toms were fighting for the best vantage points. As he got closer, he could see there were a large number of cats inside. Some appeared terrified, but most of them seemed happy just to be out of the rain.

He quickly did an informal count. He figured there were at least twenty-five cats in this old abandoned facility. *It shouldn't be too difficult to make friends,* Caterwaul thought to himself. *But where am I to find a solid-white cat? All of these have colors or some sort of markings on them.*

It was true. He even noticed what he thought to be a

completely hairless cat. He'd never seen one of those before; one of the other cats called it a Sphynx. But it didn't look entirely real to him. He was sure it was some kind of prank. Caterwaul looked around for hours, but saw no pure-white cats at all.

Even here, where he'd hit upon the highest concentration of potential contestants, he'd struck out. There was not a single pure-white animal, female or otherwise, to be found. There was one that looked like it might be suitable, but on close inspection he saw that she had a black spot on her nose and another one on her left ear. Apart from that though, she was quite charming.

When the storm subsided, the cats inside the building scattered. There were kitties to meet and places to be, after all. Caterwaul thought he would take the time to explore the large and now empty facility. It appeared to be a deserted blacksmith's shop. He assumed this because there were many tools, such as hammers and anvils, lying about.

There was a forge for heating metal and devices that smiths used for shaping it. Most of the items looked to be in workable condition, and Caterwaul could not understand why all of this was just abandoned. *What had happened here,* he wondered?

Then it dawned on him. *That chattering fool of a rat, Edsel. He had been a blacksmith, hadn't he?* At least Caterwaul thought that was what he remembered the rodent having said. But then Edsel said a lot of things, most of which were untrue. However, this time it made sense. This had been his place. The word must have gotten out that the Witch had cursed the place and taken him away. So, the mouthy little pest was telling the truth after all.

As he examined Edsel's facility, Caterwaul heard what sounded like a heated argument. He crept toward the sound of the voices. There, just inside the fence of what must have once been a horse paddock, he spotted an obese, gray-and-white youngster that had a smaller kitten cornered against the gatepost.

"You call that food?" the fat kitten squawked. He stood over what looked like a piece of the ravaged carcass of a pigeon or some other bird. Whatever it once was in life, it was now only yellowish bones long picked clean of its tasty bits. His fat face pressed close to the little fellow's, and gobs of cat spit flew onto the cornered youth. "How am I s'posed to eat that? I want real food." He swung his fat paw and struck the little guy in the head, knocking him over. "Go and bring me back something I can really sink my teeth into."

It was obvious to Caterwaul that he was witnessing a cat shakedown here. The bigger kitten was literally throwing his weight around. The smaller kitten looked weak and emaciated, and he was obviously terrified. Caterwaul wanted to intervene, but he didn't want to rush in without knowing what was going on backstage. Bullies like the gray-and-white rarely operated alone.

The gray-and-white was a kitten still, but looked to be almost as large as Caterwaul. He was sure that he could take the fat cat, providing he could make the fight last. He knew the obese kitten would tire and then it would be over. But if there were a whole group of them lurking close by, the outcome would be different. Because of this, Caterwaul chose caution.

Slipping out of his pack, he searched for a good place to hide it. There was enough food to last him for several days, and considering these circumstances, he did not care to lose it. But there were other things in the pack, besides the food, that he was really fearful of losing: the elements he needed to perform his array of spells and enchantments. He hid the pack under a pile of leaves and straw to keep it safe.

He crept closer. Perched on a rotten old sawhorse, he scoured the area visually for signs that the gray-and-white might have accomplices. Sure enough, hidden in the tall grass not ten feet away were two other young tomcats. One of them was a gray-and-black stripy of medium build, and the other one was larger and marked over most of its fur with yellow blotches. Both cats looked as if they had seen a few fights. The stripy was covered with scars, and the big yellow cat had a droopy eye and was missing a major piece of his right ear.

They were both staying out of sight, ready to jump in if there was any trouble. If he had a prayer of helping the tiny cat, he would have to create some form of diversion to draw the other two cats away. Only with them out of play could he move against the gray-and-white.

The obese kitten grabbed the smaller one by the scruff of its neck. There was plenty of loose skin. The smaller kitten was obviously starving. Caterwaul returned to where he had stashed his pack and removed from it a small pouch made of folded paper. Tucking it into his collar, he moved to outflank the hidden cats, hoping to come at them from the behind.

Caterwaul knew that he probably stood little chance against the two of them, but he had a plan he hoped would work. He moved out in a semicircle of about one hundred yards, and then made a beeline to a spot some twenty feet behind where the cats were concealed. He then proceeded to thrash about in the tall grass making sure to create as much noise as possible. The hidden cats moved to see what the ruckus was about.

Up on his toes in a fighting stance, he issued his challenge. Caterwaul's tail and fur were up and at attention as he hissed at the two, who continued moving toward him defiantly. He was confident that at least one of them would strike at his throat.

Leaping toward the onrushing cats, Caterwaul drew in a deep breath and struck out with his claws bared. He landed on the back of the big yellow and struck at its head. His momentum from the jump, however, caused him to miss and he was easily shaken off, landing on his back on the ground.

At that instant, the scarred-up stripy made his move. This was obviously the leader of the two. He flashed his teeth at Caterwaul, who noticed that his incisors were bigger than they should have been. They appeared to him like daggers.

As Caterwaul predicted, the stripy slashed for his neck. The cat's claws tore directly into the paper pouch, tearing it open and releasing its contents. Once exposed to the air, the contents produced a bright flash. A cloud of dust and smoke filled the air around them. Off balance and breathing in the fumes, both the stripy and the big yellow staggered a bit, lost their balance, and fell over unconscious.

Caterwaul dashed away from the cloud before daring to draw air again. He raised his paw to his neck, checking his injury. It was bleeding, but not too badly. The stripy cat's claws had only scratched him.

"That was lucky," he muttered to himself.

Making sure both cats were unconscious, he followed his semicircular path back to where the gray-and-white had been harassing the little one. The fat kitten was sitting there still sucking imaginary meat from the bird skeleton, but there was no sign of his victim anywhere. Nevertheless he was making some truly disgusting sounds as he sucked at bare bones, and it grossed Caterwaul out.

Obviously the intimidation of the gray-and-white had worked, and the smaller cat was off looking for more food for his tormentor.

"Are you going to eat all that yourself, fatso?" Caterwaul asked sarcastically. The gray-and-white kitten turned toward Caterwaul and let what might have been a wing joint drop to the ground.

"Who in the world are you?" asked the fat kitten.

"You're really good at smacking around the little guys aren't you? Want to tangle with me?" Caterwaul hissed, and he drew his claws.

"What do you care about it?" answered the gray-and-white as he unsheathed his own. "It's my business."

As the gray-and-white moved closer toward him, Caterwaul could see he had misjudged this other animal's size. Though still technically a "kitten," the gray-and-white was actually much larger than he had previously estimated, and easily had five pounds on Caterwaul.

"If I were you, I would go about my business, stranger. Don't you know who I am? If not, my name is Lucius . . . and this here is my patch of ground."

Caterwaul leaped toward Lucius, and the larger cat dodged. He was much quicker than Caterwaul had anticipated, especially for a fat kitty. Caterwaul leaped up into the air and came down on a fence rail. He turned around just in time to see the gray-and-white's left paw strike him across the cheek. Caterwaul stumbled a second before regaining his balance. He clambered up a post to the top rail of the fence.

Lucius spryly followed him up the post. He was much more conditioned than he looked. His fat belly shook from side to side, but it did not seem to slow him down.

As Caterwaul ran along the top of the paddock fence, the bad cat continued his pursuit. Caterwaul opened up some distance between them. Finally it seemed his opponent was running out of steam. Up ahead, he could see a large sycamore tree with some low-hanging branches. He wondered if the tree's seedpods were ready to fall.

He thought back to his time in the forest. He remembered how he used to like to throw the seed pods of the sycamore at Edsel. The pods contained seeds, which when ripened, produced fibers that caused uncontrollable itching upon contact with fur or skin. Caterwaul had always called it "itchy powder." He would laugh as the fibers clung almost magnetically to the rat's greasy coat. He hoped this tree's pods were ready to drop. Some itchy powder would come in handy right about now.

Caterwaul hopped from the fence rail onto a low-hanging tree limb and sprinted up its length to the trunk. He hurried to a set of branches that looked promising, and he carefully eased along one. It was no good. The tree had pods, but they weren't yet ripe. They were hard and spiky and green. The fibers had not yet appeared.

"Maybe I can use them anyway," thought Caterwaul. He stretched his paw out to grab one and the branch began to bend. It wasn't thick enough to hold his weight. As the branch dipped downward, he grabbed at one of the pods just as he lost his footing.

"Don't let me fall, please don't let me fall," he said aloud to himself. It was all he could think of. Amazingly, he was able to recover his balance and slid back up toward the tree trunk, pod in paw.

Bouncing from the trunk to the thickest branch he could find, Caterwaul shot along its length to a place above where Lucius was. The gray-and-white was sitting on the top rail below him. He looked exhausted and his massive form trembled as he sucked at the elusive air.

"If you're still hungry, why don't you try eating this?" Caterwaul threw the unripe spiked seedpod at the cat, hitting him square in the face. The attack knocked him off balance. It was then that Caterwaul pounced, and both of the cats tumbled to the ground. They were screaming loudly as they fought, claws slashing at each other, fur flying from the blows.

Soon it was over. The defeated Lucius was laid out on his back on the ground with Caterwaul sitting on his chest, claws out. Gasping for breath, the defeated fat cat cried out for his companions, "Bugsy, Meyer," he gasped. "Come quickly. I need you."

"If you are looking for your two goon buddies, they won't be coming."

Lucius looked stunned and terrified.

"I already took care of those two earlier, so they won't be helping you any time soon." Caterwaul sneered. "If I were you, I would go and find you another patch to work. This one isn't yours anymore.

"Now get out of here."

He climbed from atop the shaking wad of fur and snarled at him. The defeated cat limped off.

Gerhard

Caterwaul searched for signs of the little kitten, but found none. He couldn't have gotten far, Caterwaul thought. After about an hour with no results, he thought it best to get back to his assignment.

He looked around until the sun started to go down, but there were still no signs of a white cat. He felt good about his performance in the fight earlier in the day. He had used all of his abilities—physical, mental, and magical—in the contest and was victorious.

He was very tired now, though. He found himself a nice stoop and curled up underneath it. His wounds had stopped bleeding, but he could see there were spots where pieces of his fur coat were missing. They had been ripped out in the fight. "That's going to really impress the girls," he sighed.

He was fortunate that he'd remembered to pack a makeshift first-aid kit. Some salve made from garlic juice and dried geranium flowers would assure that his cuts would heal quickly and not become infected. He thanked his lucky stars that he had been able to study herbs while living with the Witch.

He also remembered that he was hungry. Reaching into his pack, he withdrew a piece of dried fish that Orris had given him. He truly loved dried carp. It was one of his favorite meals. As Caterwaul prepared for dinner, he made sure that he cleaned his fur and paws extra carefully. He didn't want to have any stray bits of Lucius contaminating his dinner.

He was just about to start eating when he heard a feint meow. Wheeling about he spied the small kitten peering at him from one of the bushes near the stoop. The kitten had snuck up on him silently. This was not good, he thought. The kitten was also shaking. He was obviously afraid.

"Hey little guy, don't be scared," Caterwaul said softly. "I won't hurt you, I promise." He motioned with his paw for the kitten to come forward.

The kitten hesitated. He wasn't used to anyone being nice to him.

"Do you want some fish?" Caterwaul asked. He reopened his pack and pulled out another piece of the dried carp. "You look hungry. Come on over here and have some food. I have plenty and can't eat all this by myself."

The kitten was still unsure, so Caterwaul pushed the second piece of fish forward and withdrew several paces. "Come on now. You can have it. No tricks . . . I promise you." The little cat cautiously moved toward the piece of fish. When he saw that Caterwaul remained at a distance, he leaped on it and started tearing at it ravenously, like he hadn't eaten anything in days.

"There you go," said Caterwaul. "It's pretty good, no?" The kitten nodded his head repeatedly while he gorged himself. "Hey now, little guy, slow down," Caterwaul laughed. "There is plenty. No one is going to take it away from you."

"What's your name boy?" asked Caterwaul.

"Coy," said the kitten without pausing. "My name is Coy. This is really good. I haven't had fish in a long time."

Caterwaul found that hard to believe. "But there is a river which runs through Harsizzle less than a mile from here.

There are fishermen and merchants all over this town."

"Not anymore, there aren't," said the kitten. "You have noticed that there are a lot more cats running around these parts lately? A whole lot of them used to be fishermen. But a little while ago, all of the fishermen turned into cats. You see people can't look into mirrors anymore. If they do, they get turned into cats, like us . . . Poof! It happens just like that."

He finished up his piece of fish. "I don't suppose you have any more you can spare?"

Caterwaul nodded and pushed the uneaten portion of his own dinner toward the starving kitten. "So how does that affect the fishermen?" he asked.

"Well," Coy responded in an almost matter of fact way. "The water in the river is not perfectly clear, see? Like most rivers it has a greenish-brown tint. Because of this, the river's surface is reflective. The fishermen went down to the river to work one day, and then all of a sudden, they turned into cats. It was like the whole river became a giant mirror . . . Scary was what it was."

He wolfed down a large mouthful of the carp. "So, as you can imagine, no more fisherman means the number of fish in Harsizzle becomes significantly reduced. And what fish do manage to come out of the river these days are strictly controlled by the Felinos."

Caterwaul hadn't considered that other reflective surfaces might also have been affected by his spell. He would have to find a way to address that type of collateral damage before using it again.

"In fact, there is a serious shortage of all types of food in the village these days, not just fish. Why with all these newcomers running around town, producing nothing, the rodent population has disappeared as well."

Taking another mouthful of his food, Coy continued, "Most

cats these days round here are glad just to get some scraps out of the trash of the few remaining humans, or from picking the bits off the rotting carcasses of dead things they find lying about. Things were so much better before, when there were just a few of us in town."

Caterwaul was ashamed. He had caused this. It was entirely his fault. He needed to find the white female and get back so he could lift the spell. "Who are these Felinos you mentioned?" he asked the youth.

"You're kidding me, right?" asked the small cat sarcastically. "You haven't heard of the outfit? The organization? The Felino family? The mob? The Felinos . . . they're gangsters.

"They have complete control of the docks. They operate out of their power base down at the riverfront. Come to think of it, they control almost all the cat rackets around here. If it's crooked, then you can bet that you'll find a Felino has got his filthy little paws in it.

"You must be new in town if you don't know who the Felinos are. You know that gray-and-white chunkster you fought a little while ago? He's one of them . . . He's a pretty important underboss in the outfit too."

He finished up the last of his fish. "Wow, I thought every cat knew about the Felinos?"

"So . . . you saw all that then, did you?" Caterwaul asked.

"Of course," said Coy. "I was hiding near where you stashed your bag. Don't worry, I didn't take anything . . . I swear it. I wasn't about to steal from anyone nuts enough to take on Lucius Jr. But hey . . . just so you know, your hiding place was pretty obvious. A big pile of leaves and hay? Come on . . . if I was trying to nab your stuff that pile would have been the first place I'd have looked.

"By the way, thank you for your timely intervention. That fat cat has been shaking me down ever since we were weaned. But I am curious about one thing, though. How did you get rid of Meyer and Bugsy? Lucius Jr. doesn't go anywhere without his muscle. They couldn't have been more than ten feet away when fatso was slapping me around. The pig likes his audience, you see. So . . . what did you do to 'em?"

"That's a long story for another day," said Caterwaul as he prepared to go to sleep. "I'm bushed."

Coy suddenly became seriously concerned. "You know they're gonna come after you, right? By now Lucius Jr. has told his old man what you did to him, and the whole family will be out looking for you. The family doesn't like it when outsiders mess with their action or their people. If I was you, I would leave town quick-like. I'm sure there's already a price on your tail."

But Caterwaul didn't hear him. He was already out cold, the rigors of the day having taken their toll. He was sound asleep, slipping into dreams of goldfish, scratching posts, and large balls of string. The little cat curled up next to him, and he also fell asleep.

~

The next morning Caterwaul awoke to the sound of a dog barking. He looked around for Coy, but the little guy was nowhere to be seen. He peered out from beneath the stoop and saw a pair of human legs. They were the legs of a hunter. Running about sniffing the ground was a large hound.

"Sic 'em, boy," shouted the man. "Chase those cats outta here. Durn cats are everywhere. They're nothing but a durn nuisance. The whole town's starting to stink. It's turning into a flipping cat box." Cats scampered away from the onrushing dog. Caterwaul made the man for a hunter. He wore tan linen pants and a deerskin jacket. On his back was a quiver of arrows and he had a short bow slung over one shoulder. In a sheath on his belt was a large knife.

Caterwaul remained hidden until the hunter and his beast were out of sight and then started down the road in the opposite direction. He continued to look for the white female cat for most of the day, but had no luck. He was trying to stay inconspicuous. He was thinking about what Coy had said about the Felinos. There was no sense in taking any unnecessary risks.

While he was looking, he spotted a grove containing three more sycamore trees. Glancing around underneath the canopy, noted that their seed pods were more mature than those of the tree down at the blacksmith's. He searched the ground and found five pods ready to release their seeds. "Thank you, Mrs. Sycamore, for your generous gift. These ought to come in handy." He stripped the seeds from the pod into a piece of paper he found lying on the ground and put them into his pack for safekeeping.

Several long hours later, Caterwaul was ready to give up and move on to the next village. Just then he glanced down an alleyway and noticed a cat rummaging through some garbage. He appeared to be quite hungry. His body was a pale gray, and he had deep blue eyes. His paw markings were considerably lighter than the rest of him, and this gave the impression that he was wearing little white boots. On his head was a cap that looked like one the foreign sailors wear, only smaller, like it had been taken off a child's doll.

Caterwaul thought the fellow looked funny in his sailor's cap. "Ahoy there, mate," he shouted jokingly as he approached the trash bin. "I am Caterwaul, and I'm new in town. I was wondering if you could tell me where I might be able to meet some ladies of class?"

"Sure mate, I came in on a ship a few weeks ago. Name's Gerhard, at your service. Would you care for a fish head? They're really quite delicious after they've had a chance to sit in the sun awhile and have been properly seasoned, of course." In his paw the gray cat held a decaying fish head. The smell was horrendous.

"No thank you, my friend," said Caterwaul trying not to breathe. "Although I am sure that you are a connoisseur of fish heads," he swished his paw to chase away the congregating flies. "I'm not particularly hungry. But please, you go ahead and enjoy it."

"Ladies, eh?" asked the gray cat, getting back to the point as he jumped to the ground. He still held onto the rotten fish head. "There's more than a few in the village, I tell you." He took a huge bite of his snack. "What're you looking for?"

"Just out for a bit of fun," said Caterwaul.

"Oh fun, eh?" he laughed. "That might be harder to find. Not much of that around these parts, at least not lately." As he spoke, he must have allowed a piece of the head to slide down his windpipe because he started choking. He coughed several times as if trying to dislodge a hairball. Caterwaul moved forward to help, but the other cat waved him off as if to say he was all right.

"I'm good," he said, looking like his eyes were about to pop out of his head. "It appears, my friend, that we have both come to a town that's experiencing a food shortage of sorts." He hopped toward Caterwaul. "Name's Gerhard," the cat repeated, offering his outstretched paw. There were fish guts clinging to his fur and Caterwaul hesitated to grab it.

"Oh sorry, mate," said Gerhard, shaking the residue from his paw. He again offered it, and this time, since it had much less goo on it, Caterwaul shook.

"I'm Caterwaul," he said grasping the grimy paw.

"As it happens, my fine feline friend, I too have been drawn here by the lure of the fairer sex. I stowed away on a boat and came here. Now I know what you're thinking. Why would a good-looking geezer like myself, who obviously could have his pick of the litter, so to speak, when it comes to the ladies, need to sneak on board some dodgy watercraft and come all this way to a foreign place in search of love?"

Putting his paw to the side of his mouth, he whispered softly, "I heard that this Harsizzle place was just crawling with females."

He grabbed up what was left of his fish head. "Sure you don't want any mate?" he asked. "I'm telling you, you don't know what you're missing. It's very tasty. I can't offer you the eyeballs though. I already ate them. I can't help myself. I just love the eyeballs. I always eat them first," he laughed as he took another mouthful. "It's too bad they only have the two."

Caterwaul started to wretch. "The females," he said trying not to vomit. "You were talking about the females."

Gerhard grinned. There was a tiny piece of rotten fish caught in his teeth. Then he noticed the look of disgust on Caterwaul's face. "Oy," he asked, "before I say another word, are you a real cat or did you look into one of those bloody mirrors?" he asked.

"No, I am all cat, one of a litter of six," Caterwaul assured him.

"It's all straight then. I was worried there for a minute. You were acting like a cat on hot bricks, if you know what I mean."

Caterwaul wasn't quite sure what Gerhard was talking about, but remained silent.

"It appears that quite a few new additions to the species have been caused by mirrors recently. I'm sure you've noticed. That's the reason there's no food. It's a population explosion, and it's totally throwing off the ratio, if you know what I mean." He winked at Caterwaul. "Not that I've had any trouble scoring, mind you.

"And when it comes to the ladies, my friend, I happen to be quite partial to the big ones," he continued. "They just look healthy, you know. I like my women to have some meat on their bones, if you know what I mean. Small ankles and a hefty frame, that's good breeding you, know." Gerhard nibbled a little bit of his fish head. "What kind of girls do you fancy?"

"I am partial to white cats. I mean pure white, the kind with no markings. I have always loved how their coats glimmer in the snow. They really take my breath away. Any chance you have seen any pure-white cats around here?" Caterwaul asked him.

"No, mate. I can't say I have." He started thinking about how it might be nice to meet a really big all-white cat, and a dreamy smile came over his face.

Caterwaul was disappointed. He thought this Gerhard might have been able to help. It seemed that he would have to continue searching.

"But there's gonna be a mixer up at the old windmill just three days from now. Do you know where that is?" Gerhard sat down and started cleaning himself.

"No, I don't," replied Caterwaul. "Where is this old windmill?"

"It's up on old man Farrow's farm, about a kilometer northwest of the village. It's a really happening place. They hold these shindigs pretty regularly. Lots of females will be there. It's usually invite-only, but a handsome geezer such as yourself ought to have no problem getting in. If they hold you up, drop my name. I know a few of the folks who are putting on this little soiree."

He finished cleaning his paws and held them up as if to ask Caterwaul if he had done a thorough enough job. "The birds will be all over you like catnip, trust me. You might even bag you a white one, if you play your cards right." He turned as if to leave, then looked back toward Caterwaul.

"I believe it starts up around nightfall. You'll be able to hear the music as you get close. One good thing about humans turning into cats is that some of them were musicians before they had four legs. They can't play quite as well as they used to, but the owners of the place get 'em dirt cheap . . . they work for scraps," said Gerhard, laughing loudly, overly impressed with his own joke.

"Thank you Gerhard," said Caterwaul. "I hope our paths cross again. May we both find what we're looking for."

"That would be positively electric, my friend," Gerhard yelled over his shoulder. He hopped down the street in the direction of the river.

Caterwaul was spent. There were still a few more hours left of daylight, but he had run himself ragged scouring the town searching for the white cat. The queen demanded results, but so far he had nothing. He felt that his best chance of success was to attend this party at the old windmill.

Now if he could only stay out of the way of the Felinos until then. He shook his head and smiled nervously. It would be difficult. Still they weren't his biggest worry. He dreaded more what might happen to him if he were to return to the castle empty-handed.

13

A White Cat

Caterwaul decided it would in his best interests to lay low for a couple of days. After all, he still had plenty of food. All he had to do was stay out of sight. But where was there to hide? He was pretty sure that most of the good spots were probably taken. Plus he worried that the hunter and his dog might return.

He didn't want to follow Gerhard. The sailor cat was heading down toward the riverfront, and that meant Felinos. He decided to make for the old windmill. He might get lucky and find a good spot to hide along the way.

He was glad to find that most of the grass around him was quite high and about to go to seed. This provided him with excellent cover. He looked quite like a panther, stalking, as he moved through it. In a couple of hours, when the sun went down, his black coat would make him nearly invisible.

Up ahead in the distance, Caterwaul heard a loud, shrill squawking sound. Something out of the ordinary was definitely going on. As he neared the source, he became extra cautious. But he was a cat, after all, and naturally curious. Carefully he edged toward the commotion. Then he saw what was making the racket. Up in a tree, not twenty feet away, was a bird's nest with three hungry babies inside. But it wasn't the chicks that were causing the ruckus. It was the momma. She was swooping down from the sky with the precision of a dive-bomber. On the ground, facing the tree was her target: a solid-white cat.

But was it a female? Caterwaul couldn't tell. It was starting to become dark. He figured the sun would be down very soon, probably within the hour. The momma bird was getting closer to the intruder with each pass. This was no sparrow or chickadee either. It was a starling, and she was angry. The white cat covered its head with its front paws, but brazenly remained. Hunger can sometimes make one brave— or desperately stupid.

The momma starling wheeled about for another pass. Shrieking all the way she plunged, talons bared. This time she struck the white cat squarely between the shoulders. The cat squealed and took off running with the angry bird pursing until it was safely out of sight. She then returned to guarding her nest.

Steering clear of the angry mother, Caterwaul followed the fleeing cat. This was the first all-white one that he had seen since leaving the castle. It had to be a female. It just had to. He was afraid, though, that it had gotten away from him. What horrible luck.

Then in the distance, he spotted it. It sure looked as if it was pure white. It was a fast animal. He had to run what he imagined was the length of three village streets to catch up. Not wanting to be seen just yet, he watched the cat slip silently into a barn.

Tiptoeing carefully up to the barn door so as to not make any noise, Caterwaul peered around the corner. Right in front of him, not five yards away, was the all-white cat. It looked like it was stalking something. He pulled his head back because he didn't want to reveal himself, at least not just yet. "There must be another way in," he thought aloud.

Looking around on the side of the barn, he saw a window.

It was high up on the south wall, but it was open. He praised his good luck. Fortunately for him, there was also a fairly tall oak near the barn with a number of branches extending in the direction of the opening.

Climbing quickly up the tree, Caterwaul bounced along its branches until he was within jumping distance of the window. It was still a stretch, but he thought he could make it. He hopped up and down on the branch to get it swaying. Then he launched himself at the open portal, hoping that the upward movement of the tree limb might add some extra distance to his leap. Landing awkwardly in a pile of straw, he prayed he hadn't given himself away.

He hadn't. He was far enough above the ground, and the white cat was too involved in its own affair to notice his less-than-smooth landing. *Excessive high living*, he thought. His time at the castle had done nothing for his stealthiness. He decided to hang back awhile and observe.

It was obvious the white cat was after something. But what was it? Caterwaul couldn't tell. Whatever it was, it was located on the ground under the storage platform where he was hiding. He searched about the platform for a knothole. He was lucky. There were several. He moved to the closest one and put his eye next to it. Then he saw what it was that so interested the cat. On the ground, directly beneath him, was a wounded mouse, thrashing about in the hay.

The hungry white cat was focused on what appeared to be an easy meal. Because of this, it did not see what Caterwaul could from his elevated position. The mouse was bait in a trap. Just an inch in front of the rodent, partially covered in hay, was a piece of dull metal, which had been rigged to trigger a containment device of some type. Before Caterwaul could shout a warning, the trap sprung. The snare was a primitive one, made of a few springs, some wood and hemp cloth, but it was effective. It caught the white cat completely by surprise.

The cat was howling wildly. "Got us another one boy," said an excited voice. Caterwaul shifted position in order to determine the source. It was the hunter and his dog, but this time, he had not been content just to chase the cats away. Emerging from the darkness, the hunter picked up his trap and headed toward the barn door. The captive feline continued to shriek.

Caterwaul remained motionless until the man and his canine companion were gone. "Now what am I going to do?" he asked himself. He ran back to the open window to see which way the two were heading. He had to follow them. This was the only white cat he had seen since leaving Druciah's castle. He wasn't going to mess this up. He needed to find where the man was taking it.

Leaping onto some bales of hay below, Caterwaul hit the ground running. He tore out of the barn after the hunter. Following the man was not going to be easy. He had to make sure he remained far enough behind to avoid being detected by the hound. Fortunately there were now so many felines in Harsizzle that the huge number of overlapping scents had the poor dog befuddled.

He remained at a safe distance, watching. Soon the man and his beast came to a large house. Behind the house was a utility building, like a woodshed only larger and built more sturdily. The approach to the house was bare and rocky and dotted with large muddy areas that had yet to dry from the previous day. Caterwaul no longer had the advantage of the tall grass, so he remained hidden.

The hunter set the trap down at the bottom of a small set of stairs and walked up into the house. He emerged a minute later without his bow and quiver. He walked toward a chain, which was wrapped around a tree and hooked it to the dog's collar.

Caterwaul eased closer to the building. It was now dark

outside so his courage was up, despite the presence of the hound. He was sure he could hear the sound of cats, many cats, coming from the outbuilding.

The man picked the trap up again and started toward the sounds. When he got up to the door, he set the trap down again and lit a torch. He unlocked the door and opened it. As it swung open Caterwaul saw what looked like dozens of similar traps stacked one on top of the other. Each one of them contained a trapped cat.

"Pssst . . . What the heck are you doing?" a voice called to him. It was Coy, the kitten he had saved from Lucius Jr. Again he had slipped right on up to Caterwaul without him noticing.

"That hunter has cats in there," answered Caterwaul. "From what I could see when he opened the door, it looks like he's holding a lot of us in there."

"No kidding," said Coy. "He's been out rounding up cats all over town. Most of us know to stay out of his way. He hates cats. He usually just sends his dog Huxley to chase after us. But something different is going on here." Coy motioned for Caterwaul to follow him.

"Word on the streets is someone made a deal with him to round us all up and get rid of us."

"Who do you think . . . the Felinos?" Caterwaul asked.

"Not their style." They stopped and crouched down behind a large stone. "Besides, the Felinos like having all these cats around. It makes their job easier. They can pretty much make a cat do whatever they want now. They control the fish stocks. It's a supply-and-demand thing. If the cats go bye-bye, so does their influence. Nah . . . It's definitely not the Felinos. I'm thinking it's gotta be a human."

Before Caterwaul could ask who, the door to the building opened again and the hunter came out. Coy put his claw to his lips, motioning for silence. Caterwaul pressed his body close to the ground. They waited for the man to go back into the house before daring to move an inch.

"Okay, let's go," said Coy.

"Go where? What's the plan?"

"You and me are gonna take us a closer look at that building," the kitten answered.

If there was one skill the little cat had mastered, it was how to move about silently. Not a single leaf rustled or twig snapped as he moved toward the outbuilding. Caterwaul was jealous. He had always considered himself pretty sneaky, but compared to Coy, he was a rank amateur. He tried to do what the little cat did, but he did not even begin to come close.

Still they made it to the building without attracting the attention of Huxley the hound. The big lug's attention was thoroughly drawn away by a rather large bone. Caterwaul suspected it was a part of a deer leg. The hound smiled and slobbered as he gnawed away, oblivious to their presence.

"Help me," said Coy straining, "I want to try to dig away at the dirt under the back wall. My paws are too small to do it on my own."

Caterwaul got down in the dirt and proceeded to help him dig. Soon they had removed enough dirt to make a hole large enough for Coy to squirm through. A few moments later, the smaller cat emerged.

"I counted twenty-eight cats and two more empty cages," said Coy. "So it looks like the inn is pretty much booked. Whoever is behind this is probably going to come by in the next few days to pick them all up.

"That means if we are going to do anything to free these cats, we have to do it now."

Caterwaul nodded in agreement. "So what do we do?"

"I have an idea," said Coy, "but it's pretty dangerous. Come here." Coy moved close and whispered something in his ear. Caterwaul removed his pack and took something from it.

A few minutes later, he was moving toward where the dog lay chewing on his bone. Caterwaul quietly estimated the length of the chain. This was going to be tricky. He wasn't sure if he was quick enough to pull it off.

He shimmied up behind the clueless hound. The noises coming from the dog's chewing were more than enough to cover any he would make. He hoped that the aroma of the venison marrow would similarly mask his scent.

Placing his left forelimb on a short stump, Caterwaul raised his front end up and hurled something at the hound. It was an acorn, but unlike most acorns, this one was full of a powder designed to explode on impact. The seed hit Huxley square in the butt and flashed.

Boom! The drooling hound shot to attention, howling in pain. He whirled about to see what had caused his discomfort. There, leaning against the stump, he spotted Caterwaul, who waved at him. "Hi there," the cat said.

Huxley snarled and grinned. He was pretty fast. Caterwaul was surprised to find out just how fast the dog was. He snapped his frothy jaws, barely missing the fleeing feline. The dog was also huge. Caterwaul thought: *He must weigh eighty pounds or more.* Also he noted that a good percentage of the dog's total body weight was his head, which despite its jowliness and generally amicable appearance, was full of sharp and scary teeth.

Caterwaul knew his only real advantage here was his agility. Roused as he was to anger, the dog would likely be off-balance. Caterwaul did a quick stutter-step, stopped, and dodged left abruptly, causing the hound to hurtle past him. He then jetted around the side of the building with the dog close on his heels. He could feel the dog's hot breath on his tail. Summoning the last of his strength, he shot forward.

He imagined he was a cheetah or one of the other giant cats he had heard about. He propelled himself through the air, extending his body like an athlete in competition. When his paws touched down, he prayed he'd reached a place safely out of Huxley's reach.

The chain on the dog went taut. He had guessed right. Huxley's head snapped back and he fell over, yelping as he reached the end of the chain's length. Taking no chances, Caterwaul took off. He did not stop until he was out of the dog's sight. The next part was all on Coy.

As the hound regained his footing, Coy shot from behind his rock and made straight for the hole, which he and Caterwaul had been digging under the wall. He made sure this time to make as much commotion as he could so the dog would follow. He squeezed through the gap seconds before Huxley arrived at the spot.

Not to be out maneuvered again, the dog started digging furiously at the hole. He was barking very loudly and howling as the dirt flew into the air behind him. He made so much noise that the hunter came running out of the house.

"What in the world is going on out here?" he shouted at the beast. But Huxley was oblivious to his master's presence. He continued digging wildly. The hole was now almost big enough for the hound to get through. He was going to get that cat. It was the only thing on his mind. The hunter was shouting at him, but he couldn't hear. The imprisoned cats wailed frantically in their cages at the commotion outside.

"Durn it, Huxley, I said stop it." The hunter grabbed the chain and yanked the dog away from the hole. Huxley yelped as the collar he was wearing pulled tightly against his windpipe. He was choking. "Now look what you've done. I'm going to have to come out here tomorrow and fill that blasted ditch back in."

He smacked the dog repeatedly across his rump. He did this with an open hand, but it was very hard. Huxley yelped, whimpered, and slunk away, shaking. "What in blazes is wrong with you?" Unhooking him from the chain, he grabbed the animal by the collar and dragged him inside the house.

Once things had quieted down, Caterwaul came slinking back. Coy's plan had worked perfectly. The dog's frantic digging increased the size of the opening tenfold. The gap under the wall was now enormous. There was easily more than enough room for two or three cats to get through at the same time.

Caterwaul stuck his head through the gap and looked around, but he saw no sign of Coy. He was about to call the little cat's name when Coy tapped him on his shoulder.

"Come on. Let's get outta here for a while. We'll come back in an hour or so, when things have had a chance to calm down." Coy looked at Caterwaul and started to laugh. "Man," he said chuckling, "That was way too close for comfort. If that hunter hadn't come out when he did, I might be a chew toy right now." As they left the yard, they did not notice that Huxley was watching them from a window in the house.

About ninety minutes later, they returned. Coy felt that enough time had passed. They scoured the yard for signs of Huxley but there were none. The angry hunter had the hound locked up safely inside the house.

Coy scurried through the hole, and Caterwaul followed. Sure enough the inside of the building was filled with cages containing some very frightened cats. The cats started meowing when they saw the newcomers.

"Shhhhh," said Caterwaul, urging them to silence. "We've come to get you all out of here, but you have to be quiet. We don't want to attract attention."

A hush came over the animals, and the room was still. Coy started climbing up to the top row of cages. "Now, as we get you out, we need you to try to remain as quiet as possible and help us to free the others," the smaller cat instructed them.

They'd only had enough time to get four of the traps open when they heard the sound of horses coming from outside.

"Okay, everybody, you're going to have to be completely still now," Caterwaul said. He turned to Coy and motioned for him to investigate. The kitten deftly slid to the ground and peered through the opening. He made a gesture with his paw for Caterwaul to come look. "Get a load of this guy," he said in a muted voice.

"Oh no," Caterwaul whispered, "I think we're in trouble." Pulling up outside the hunter's house was a large wagon pulled by a pair of horses. Less than thirty feet from where they hid, sitting on his horse, was Warwick Vane Bezel III.

14

Jailbreak

Caterwaul couldn't believe his eyes. What was the queen's secret police commander doing all the way out here? He slipped out into the darkness to investigate. The hunter emerged from the house to greet Warwick with an embrace. It seemed the two were friends, or they were at least on a somewhat friendly basis. Caterwaul didn't think it possible that anyone could really like Warwick Vane Bezel III.

Coy continued with the rescue operation. He managed to get another three cages on the top level open. Then as he hopped across a gap to open a fourth trap, he made a mistake and misjudged the distance. His left rear paw failed to make contact with a solid surface, and he began to fall.

As he dropped, he instinctively grabbed out for anything he could find to slow his descent. His claws hooked onto the bag that made up part of one of the traps, and it too toppled over. This in turn created a cascade, and several other cages began to fall. The cats in and outside of the traps started to panic and cry out en masse, resulting in a "catcophony" of noise emanating from the building. *Oh well,* Caterwaul thought, *so much for secrecy.*

"Those of you who are already free, move your tails," Coy directed them. He was in obvious pain. He'd landed hard on his back, and one of the traps had him pinned underneath. "I need one of you, preferably someone with muscle, to get this blasted cage offa me." Terrified, the small number of liberated cats all shot for the opening and took off. "No . . . Don't all of you run . . . aww nuts. Somebody's gotta help me!" he shouted. The cats that remained caged up continued shrieking. Coy thought of an expression someone once used and muttered, "I guess it's true; no good deed remains unpunished."

Caterwaul watched the hunter and the queen's commander run toward the building. He hoped that Coy had gotten out with the ones he had freed, but he wasn't sure. It was very dark and Coy was so tiny. He ran to the opening and dashed through it, just as the hunter put his key into the lock.

"Caterwaul! Get over here, I'm pinned down!" shouted Coy. Caterwaul could hear the door as it began to open. Hurling his full weight at the cage, Caterwaul shifted the trap just enough for him to pull Coy free.

"Can you run?" asked Caterwaul.

"I doubt it," said Coy. "You go on; I will see if I can hide in a crack somewhere."

Fat chance of that, thought Caterwaul. "Get up on my back and hold on tight to my collar and pack. The kitten did as he was told and wrapped his paws around the pack and collar. Caterwaul could smell a torch being lit. They had no time to lose. "Don't let go for anything. You hear me?"

Caterwaul bolted for the hole just as the hunter entered with the lit torch. He hoped they had gotten out without being seen. He could hear the hunter cursing loudly at the disordered condition of his collection of traps.

"They must have escaped through that hole," he could hear Warwick Vane Bezel III say as they slipped out of earshot.

~

"So, how many of them got free?" Warwick Vane Bezel III asked the hunter.

"Looks like around six or seven of them," the hunter answered. "It's kind of hard to tell with all this mess in here." He picked up one of the cages and replaced it where it had been. The cat inside was frightened and whimpering.

"How in the world did this happen?" he asked, looking at the queen's secret police commander. "They were all locked up tight."

"Some of these cats were humans once," the commander responded, "Is it so hard to believe that a few of them might have the skill and dexterity to escape from these flimsy traps you've devised?" He picked up one of the empty cages from where it had fallen over. "From the look of this one here, I would say it's a wonder you have any cats left at all.

"Load those you have left into the wagon," said the constable, tossing the hunter a large ring full of keys. "The smallest of those keys will open the lock on the cage you will find there. Put whatever cats you have remaining inside it. You will forgive me if I don't trust your traps." He rubbed his chin in thought. "What about white ones? Have you captured any white cats for me?"

"Just the one, and she is most definitely a beauty," the hunter answered, "just what you've been looking for, I'd say."

"Excellent," said Warwick Vane Bezel III, laughing as he rubbed his gauntleted hands together. He was pleased. There were few things he could think of that would make him happier than to be able to bring the queen back her prize before that pompous Caterwaul could.

He tossed the hunter a pouch of coins. "I hope you'll understand, but I've docked you for the ones that got away."

The hunter was visibly upset, but did not dare to question him.

Once all of the remaining felines had been moved to the cage in the back of the wagon, Warwick Vane Bezel III mounted his horse and signaled for the wagon master to follow.

~

Once he felt he was safely away, Caterwaul stopped running and helped Coy down from his back. The little guy was having a hard time breathing. The weight of the cage on his small frame had obviously taken its toll. Caterwaul hoped that he didn't have any broken bones, or worse, a punctured lung.

"So how are you holding up?" Caterwaul asked him.

"I'm alive," answered the kitten. "Glad to be away from that place. Other than that though, I feel like ten days worth of garbage that's been packed into a five-day bag." He was breathing hard, and he was obviously in a lot of pain. Still, for a little guy, Coy was tough as they come. He didn't complain at all despite his many injuries.

The brave kitten's body was bleeding in several places from the cuts and scrapes he endured trying to break the captive cats out. Caterwaul suspected he was a lot more hurt than he let on.

"I guess this means I'm on the sidelines for the second half, Coach," he joked, trying to keep up a strong façade. He found it was difficult to breathe or even to walk.

"That's alright friend," Caterwaul told him. "You've done more than I ever could've asked. We're still in this game because of you." He helped Coy to the shelter of a hollowed-out log. "I'll be back for you as soon as I can. I promise."

"Go back . . . Huxley . . . Go back and see if you can make a deal with the dog," Coy said.

"The dog? Why?" answered Caterwaul.

"I'm not sure, but I've been thinking. That dog doesn't look all that happy with his role in life right now." He groaned and shifted his position to see his friend better. "It wouldn't surprise me one bit to find him willing to switch sides."

Smiling at Coy, Caterwaul turned around and headed back down in the direction he came from. As he approached the hunter's place, Caterwaul could hear shouting and the sounds of a dog wailing in agony. He ducked his head down underneath one of the outer windowsills to listen. Inside the house, the hunter was beating Huxley unmercifully with what looked like a shoe. Peering through the glass of the window, Caterwaul could only watch as the dog tried in vain to get away. Huxley threw his legs up to cover his head with his paws as the hunter swung at him. When the hunter temporarily stopped the beating, Huxley tried to escape, whimpering and crying in pain.

"That will teach you to cost me money, you confounded animal." The abuse had escalated in the hunter's household. The hunter beat his dog repeatedly as the canine howled, trying in vain to escape the hits, scuttling around the room.

This went on for an eternity it seemed to Caterwaul, though it was probably about ten minutes. By the time the hunter finished, the dog could do nothing but lie on the ground twitching and trembling in fear.

A few moments later, the door of the house opened up and the hunter emerged, dragging his terrified dog by the collar. He hooked the dog back up to the chain and returned inside. Caterwaul could only watch as the miserable dog wept from the horrible beating he had been given by his master.

The cat wanted to go to see if Huxley was all right, but he hesitated. Caterwaul realized he was in no small part to blame for the awful beating Huxley just endured. He was afraid if he got anywhere close to the dog, Huxley might just try to gobble him up.

After mulling it over in his mind for a bit, he felt he had no choice but to act. Caterwaul moved toward where the beaten animal lay. "Hey, Huxley," he addressed the dog. "How's it going?"

The dog looked up at him sad-eyed from where he lay humbled in the grass. "Oh, it's you," he said with disgust. "What do you want?"

"Does that happen to you a lot?" Caterwaul asked. "Him hitting you like that . . . does he do that on a regular basis?"

"Not all the time," the dog answered. "Sometimes he's an all right guy. It's only when I do something that makes him mad, or if he does something stupid that he wants to blame me for, that he gets really violent." He stretched and sat up on his hindquarters. "But I'm just a dog . . . *his* dog, and he reminds me of that fact far too often."

Huxley really seemed miserable. It was like he was only showing the tip of the iceberg that was the abuse he had experienced. The sad expression on the dog's face was one of a long-term victim. He looked like he would give almost anything to be free of the hunter and this unhealthy, belligerent lifestyle. Caterwaul felt his pain and believed that the dog might be open to a deal of some sort.

"Look friend," Caterwaul began, "you and I may not have gotten off on the best footing, but I have something that I want you to consider."

Huxley crept forward, and his ears turned as if to show that he was interested in hearing what the cat had to say.

"My name is Caterwaul; perhaps you have heard the name?" He queried. "I am pretty well-connected around these parts. I work for Queen Druciah. Do you know who she is?"

Huxley nodded.

"How would you like to come to work for me?" asked the cat.

15

A Cage Full of Cats

Warwick Vane Bezel III was extraordinarily proud of himself, and why shouldn't he be? After all, he had a wagon full of cats with which he could do whatever he wanted, and he had also acquired the pure-white female that his employer demanded.

He chuckled to think that soon he would return to Castle Cathoon with the pure-white cat that the hated Caterwaul had been sent to procure. He took delight in the thought that he would get all the credit and the horrible black feline would now be out of favor with Druciah.

He rode slowly alongside the wagon full of cats. After about a half an hour, he came to a roadblock. There was a large, downed tree lying across the road. A number of cats were sitting on top of the tree. One of them was exceedingly fat and bore gray-and-white markings on his fur. As the horses slowed, Warwick glanced about to get the lay of the land. He stopped and dismounted.

"What's going on here?" he asked brazenly.

"Ah, you can speak," said the leader of the cats below him. "That's a good sign, and a point in your favor, I might add. Those cats you have there belong to me. They pay me protection money, so I suggest that you open up that cage and let 'em go or it could go ugly for ya." Two other cats stepped forward from out of the group; it was Meyer and Bugsy. The former flashed his oversized teeth at the secret policeman. My name is Lucius Felino Jr.," he said. "Perhaps you've heard of me?"

"I can't say that I have," answered Warwick Vane Bezel III defiantly. "As for me, you can just call me constable," he responded. A really sinister and twisted smile came over his face. "I believe that everyone who has ever set foot in this land has heard of me." He led his mount forward. "Fatso, you have no idea whatsoever whom you are dealing with.

"You see I am the chief of police for Queen Druciah, the ruler of all of these lands. I'm what you might call a heavy-hitter around here. In fact I just might be the heaviest hitter of them all. So my advice to you is this: clear out. Get that log out of my path now, and we will go on as if none of this unpleasantness ever happened." He snatched up Lucius Jr. by his copious neck, and held him up close to his face. "If you refuse me this request, I cannot begin to tell you how bad things will become for you, my fat Felino."

Warwick Vane Bezel III tossed Lucius, as if he was nothing but a ragdoll, in the direction of the downed tree with a rugged underhand motion. No cat could ever strong-arm him. Humiliated as never before, Lucius Jr., son of the mob boss, signaled for his men to pull the tree out of the road. This was no easy feat. It took Lucius and fifteen other cats a considerable amount of time to haul the tree away so that the wagon could pass.

The police commander smiled and thought to himself: *No cat will ever get the best of Warwick Vane Bezel III.*

~

It took no time at all for Huxley to pick up the constable's scent. After all, Warwick Vane Bezel III was traveling with a wagon full of cats. *He shouldn't be hard to detect,* thought Caterwaul.

A hound with olfactory senses as excellent as Huxley's would be sure to pick up his trail from miles away. Caterwaul rode on the dog's back.

As fast as he was, Caterwaul realized that Huxley was much better equipped to cover long distances. Since the two had come to their "arrangement," he was content to make use of the hound's obvious talents. "How much farther ahead is he?" asked Caterwaul.

"The best I can estimate," answered the dog, "we ought to catch up with him in the next ten to fifteen minutes." Huxley looked really excited. After years of living with the unappreciative hunter, he finally felt that he was really a part of something. This was a rescue operation. He howled with delight while Caterwaul clung tightly to his collar, trying his best just to hang on.

"What, I don't understand," Huxley asked him, "is why you didn't just come to me honest and forthright at the start?" He was moving very fast in pursuit of the wagon. "Why did you feel the need to throw that exploding doohickey at me? That hurt, by the way."

"Sorry about that friend," Caterwaul answered. "My companion and I needed you to do a job, and we weren't aware that you and your master were not really reading from the same script, if you catch my meaning."

Caterwaul cleared his throat. "I mean, look at it from my perspective. You're a dog and I'm a cat. Usually that makes for strange bedfellows, unless of course we grew up together. Dogs mostly chase us cats. You can't blame me for thinking you might be aligned against me."

"Fair enough," said Huxley not breaking his stride. "But what was it that made you change your mind about me?"

"That's obvious," said Caterwaul. "As I neared the house, I could hear the hunter beating you. And when I looked through

the window and saw him hitting you with that shoe . . . I . . . I
. . ." he stammered for a moment, "I just thought that no one
should be allowed to treat anyone that way. Especially when
he is your master and he is supposed to love you. I just don't
understand how anyone can . . ." his voice trailed off sadly.

He paused a solid minute before continuing, "Huxley, I
promise you this. If you stick with me, no one will ever beat you
like that again. You have my word on that." The dog howled
appreciatively and increased his speed, causing Caterwaul to
bounce up and down on his back. "Slow down, dog," he said
laughing. "You're going to knock me flying."

After what seemed like twenty minutes or so—it was hard
for Caterwaul to keep accurate time from his position on the
hound's back—Huxley slowed down and started sniffing the
ground. "There were cats here," he said, "and it looks like a lot
of them, more than just the ones we're after. Do you see all the
footprints?"

"What happened here?" Caterwaul asked.

Huxley pointed to a large hemp rope that was wrapped
around the end of a downed tree. "See that?" he asked. Someone
was trying to collect a toll, I'd wager. That someone was most
likely part of the outfit. But it didn't work out. Look . . . You
can see where they pulled the log back out of the road."

Caterwaul looked at the spot Huxley indicated. Sure
enough, the downed tree was there, just as Huxley said it was,
with the rope and everything. *This hound knows what he is
looking at,* Caterwaul thought.

"How much farther ahead is he?" asked Caterwaul.

"Not much further," the dog answered. "It looks like the
Felino family held him up a bit. We should intercept him in
less than ten minutes, give or take."

Huxley made sure Caterwaul was firmly ensconced on his
back and continued to move quickly after the police commander

and the wagon full of cats. The dog really knew his way around the forest. He turned his head back toward his passenger and said, "Hold on tight."

The dog made a left turn away from the path they had been following. He howled in delight and grinned ear to ear, confident in his command of the terrain. "I'm about to put us directly in his path," said the dog eagerly.

A few minutes later, the dog and his passenger emerged from the forest. He was back on what looked like the path they had been originally following. There were trees on both sides of the path. "Climb down off me now and go hide up in one of those trees," Huxley said. "When I stop him, you will know what to do."

Caterwaul leaped from the hound's back and scurried up a pine onto one of its low-hanging branches. Huxley started digging up the road furiously. Up in the tree, Caterwaul removed his shoulder pack. He was hoping he had enough of his sleeping powder to use on someone as large as Warwick Vane Bezel III. From his stores, he thought in all likelihood he did not. But then maybe he didn't actually have to put the commander to sleep. Perhaps it would be enough to simply confuse him.

He looked down from his tree branch. The dog had dug a good-sized trench in the road. If Warwick Vane Bezel III was not alert, then it might cause him some serious trouble. A few minutes later, the constable and the wagon came into view. Huxley made no move. He went on digging up the road. It was like he was possessed by a single thought.

Warwick Vane Bezel III, who was in no way, shape, or form an animal-lover, failed to recognize the dog as the hunter's pet. This played into Caterwaul's hands.

"You . . . dog. Move out of my way," barked the constable." Huxley continued his digging up the road, unmoved. "Did you not hear me, dog?" he asked again, shouting at the beast who barred his way. "I'm on a mission for the queen." Still, the hound ignored him and kept right on doing what he was doing.

Caterwaul grabbed what remained of the sleep powder from his pack and jumped down onto the top of the wagon cage. He hissed defiantly at the wagon master and swiped at his face. His claws connected with the flesh of the driver, and the man jumped down and ran away screaming.

Warwick Vane Bezel III swiveled about on his horse. He looked straight at Caterwaul and shouted, "You!" Drawing his sword, he swung it toward his target flat side forward in an attempt to knock the cat from his post atop the wagon. But Caterwaul dodged the blow. The commander missed, fanning the air wildly over the cat's head, the momentum from his errant swing nearly unhorsing him.

Seeing Caterwaul, the caged felines began to scream. It was as if they were collectively begging him to save them. Warwick Vane Bezel III leapt from his horse. It was at that instant that Huxley pounced. The hound grabbed the constable by his cloak and pulled him to the ground. Surprised by this sudden move, the constable lost hold of his weapon. He watched it bounce on the ground while he was driven backwards. He stumbled to the earth, the large dog snapping at his throat.

But Warwick Vane Bezel III was strong. Punching the excited hound in the snout, he pushed his attacker away and moved to regain his footing. Huxley yelped in pain and rolled over, growling at the policeman. Just then, Caterwaul launched himself from the wagon. Grasping the commander's leather, jerking with his claws, he clambered onto the angry man's shoulders.

"I don't know why you are here, Warwick, or what you intend to do with these cats, but whatever it is, it's not in accordance with my orders." He drew in a deep breath, leaned back and tore open the pouch of sleeping powder. Caterwaul unsheathed his claws and drove them into the commander's flesh. Warwick Vane Bezel screamed in pain and sucked in an enormous breath, drawing the sleeping powder deep into his lungs. Just as the cat expected, it was not nearly enough to knock him out. It was, however, enough to make him forget who he was and why he was here moving about the thickets of Harsizzle.

"Get that cage open now," shouted Huxley, "while you can." Caterwaul jumped back up onto the cart and moved toward the lock. If there was one thing he'd learned how to do, way before he'd ever encountered the Witch, it was how to pick a lock. Within moments the cage was open, and the cats scampered to escape. But where was the all-white cat?

The cage now stood empty, and still there was no sign of the white cat. Caterwaul glanced over at Warwick Vane Bezel III. He was moving about strangely, in a daze from the sleeping powder. He was staggering about in complete confusion. He was out of his mind, unaware of who he was or even where he was.

"Hey you guys . . . Under here." It was a voice coming from the front of the cart.

Caterwaul jumped back up onto the bench where the driver had previously been sitting. Underneath the bench, covered by a fine linen cloth, was one of the hunter's cages. Inside the cage was the white cat. As Caterwaul pulled the cover off of it, the cat appeared to be quite frightened.

"It's okay, my lovely," said Caterwaul. "I am here to rescue you." Caterwaul took one of his claws and sprang the latch on the trap holding the white cat.

"I appreciate it, friend," said the white cat, "but ease up on the lovely stuff, will ya? Because from where I'm sittin', you know . . . it just ain't that kind of party." Caterwaul's jaw dropped in disbelief.

"The name's Frankie," the white cat said, extending his

paw, "and I want to thank you for the rescue."

Caterwaul was deflated. He thought he had finally found his prize, only to have it pulled away at the last minute.

"I'm a singer. I'm pretty good actually. I do all the classics. You know the style. I'm what you might call a crooner. I always draw a crowd when I perform. You ever want to see me, you got free tickets for life.

"If ever I can do you a favor, just let me know. I owe you, big time!"

16

Interludes

The next morning, a very cold Warwick Vane Bezel III woke up shivering to a pounding headache. His clothes had been removed and were in a pile, neatly folded, on the wagon bench. All that remained to cover him were his well-worn, polka-dotted undershorts. He did not want to move. He hadn't felt this bad since the last time he had consumed way too much grog.

But he didn't remember drinking any spirits. Nor could he remember where he was or how he had gotten there. Most of all, he could not explain why he was practically naked and locked in a cage full of cat droppings.

He tried to reach through the cage to grab his clothes, but he could not get his hand far enough through the narrow bars. Frustrated beyond belief, he shook the cage angrily and screamed for about half an hour in the hope that someone might hear him and come set him free. But alas, no one heard, or if they did hear, no one came.

~

"So after all of that trouble, it turned out that the white cat wasn't a female after all. It was a male cat named Frankie," Caterwaul laughingly explained to Coy, who was still recovering from his injuries.

"Well, at least you were able to stop the wagon and free all of the cats," the kitten said. "I imagine right about now, word of your exploits is spreading all around Harsizzle. You're a hero, pal. Not just anyone can go up against the queen's top man and survive, much less come out the winner."

"Yes," said Caterwaul quietly. He also knew he was lucky. But if he didn't find the all-white female soon, his luck might run out.

Then he remembered what was most funny about the night before and burst out in hysterics. He swung back on his tail and rolled forward in the grass toward Coy, laughing. "You really should have been there for what happened next," Caterwaul said with an enormous smile. "Once I had freed all of the cats, as you might imagine, they were howling mad. They started to attack the constable from all directions at once. Some of them jumped up on him and started climbing their way up his clothes.

"Now, at that particular moment, Warwick Vane Bezel III was in the middle of a pretty powerful hallucination, which as it happens, was caused by my magic sleeping powder going off in his face. When the cats attacked, he didn't know what was happening. I have no idea what horrible creatures he thought were attacking him. I just know that he started freaking out like crazy.

"The next thing you know, he's tearing all his clothes off. Huxley thought that was so hilarious, he started in on him too. The old dog was barking furiously as the cats surrounded the commander. Then old Warwick Vane Bezel III climbed into the back of his own nasty old cat cage . . . and he's lying there, on the floor of the cage, shaking like he just saw a ghost." Caterwaul was laughing so hard, he started honking like a goose.

~

In her cave deep in the forest of Red Moon, the Witch rocked back and forth on her chair. In her mouth was a pipe made out of a carved and hollowed out gourd. It wasn't lit, but she chewed the stem nervously. In front of her was her grandfather's beautiful chessboard with its intricately carved pieces. Sitting on the board were almost a complete set of black pieces and only three white ones—a rook, one pawn, and the king. She had the white king in check and was about to put the hammer down on her opponent.

The Witch moved her rook down, making it impossible for the white king to escape. "Check and mate," she said. Taking her pipe in her hand, she threw it across the table at her competitor, if she could truly call him that. "You stink . . . as always," she shouted. "Edsel, tell me something . . . How is it that no matter how many times we play, you just don't seem to get any better? You are a rat. You were a two-legged rat before and now crawl around on all four, but a rat isn't a stupid animal . . . Rats are supposed to have problem-solving intelligence. So what, my greasy friend, is wrong with you? Hmmmmm? Why is it that I seem to find myself sharing my home with the world's most moronic rodent?"

Edsel the Rat dodged the gourd pipe and dropped down to the floor below the table. Not wanting to have anything else hurled at him, he scampered away and hid quietly under what passed for the Witch's couch. The rat was afraid to make even a sound, much less say a word, and for Edsel the Rat, that was next to impossible.

"Tell me, Edsel, did your mother engage in many high risk or unlawful activities while she was carrying you?"

The Witch wiped her forehead clear of perspiration. She was starting to become despondent. She had been without her cat, her companion, for months now. She wanted him . . . no, she needed him back. The thought occurred to her that the queen might be trying to weasel out on their deal. *No*, she thought, *the queen is no fool. She knows better than to welsh on a deal with me.*

The Witch looked at the remains of the slaughter staring back at her from the chessboard. She really hoped she would get her friend back soon.

~

Back at the blacksmith shop, Lucius Felino Jr. had egg on his face, both literally and figuratively. He was furious at how easily Warwick Vane Bezel III dismissed him on the road the night before. He was a Felino, and being a Felino is supposed to carry with it a certain level of respect. Lose respect, you lose control. That was what his father Lucius Sr. always said. And if the men lose their respect for you, it's extra hard to get it back.

He was so angry, he could not properly enjoy his breakfast. The yolk of his raw chicken egg covered his mouth, nose, and whiskers, and no matter how hard he tried, he just couldn't lick it all off.

"Somebody, get me a towel or something to wipe this mess off!" demanded Lucius Jr. Meyer tossed him what appeared to be a square cut from a napkin. The fat kitten dragged it over his face repeatedly. "Is it all off?" he asked. His companions nodded, and Lucius Jr. threw the towel on the ground.

Just then, there was a knock at the door. Lucius Jr. signaled for Bugsy to admit their visitor. He soon returned to the audience room, as Lucius Jr. called it, with a pale gray cat wearing a doll-sized sailor's cap.

"And to what do I owe the pleasure of this visit, Gerhard?" asked Jr.

"Afternoon, Guvnor," he said to the fat kitten underboss with a smile that went from ear to ear. "Word on the street is that you're lookin' to pay for any information regarding that constable fellow. The one who embarrassed you last night." He smiled fetidly and suddenly every cat in the room knew what he'd had for breakfast. "Well, I'm here to collect."

"If it's solid," the gray-and-white said, "I'll pay for solid, but you better not be yanking my collar, my fancy pants foreigner, or they'll be using your dried, dead body to scrub the toilets around here."

"Oh, this is diamond solid," he said. "And you won't have too much trouble finding him neither. You see, he's trapped. He's locked in the back of his own cat-catcher." He started laughing hysterically. "Can you beat that? Seems that this Caterwaul fellow pulled some kind of magic act on him, and the next thing you know, he's crying like a baby in the back of his own cage wearing nothing but his knickers."

"Caterwaul you say?" asked Lucius Jr.

Gerhard nodded.

"How well do you know this Caterwaul, my well-paid snitch friend?" Jr. motioned for Meyer to toss him a fat pouch full of money.

"Not well at all, I'm afraid," Gerhard responded, stammering. He wondered if now, of all times, he might have been better off being quiet. "I mean I only met him the one time. Said he was looking for a good time . . . You know, he wanted to know where the ladies were . . . and all that. That's pretty much all we had to say to each other."

Two cats stepped from out of the shadows. Each one grabbed Gerhard by an arm. Lucius Jr. strode to where the two were holding him.

"So where did you tell him to go, Gerhard? To find the females?" asked Lucius Jr. as he gently ran one of his claws against the fur of his captive's neck. "A respected, international lady-killer, such as you, must surely know all the best places where the fine kitties go to play."

Spit was flying from the mobster's fat face as he pushed

closer in a most threatening way. "You don't want to make your old pal Lucius upset now? Do you now, Gerhard?"

17

The Party at the Old Windmill

Just as Gerhard said he would, Caterwaul could hear the music coming from old man Farrow's farm long before he saw the building, but as the old windmill came into view, he had no doubt he had come to the right place. The joint was lit up like a storefront at Christmastime. He wondered what they had done to make the lights flash on and off and change colors the way they did.

On the outside, it looked to be a typical large windmill. It was made of granite and wood. Though hardly crude in design, it was nowhere near as intricate as Caterwaul had imagined. The renovations he had made to Cathoon, designed to his specifications, led him to expect something greater, so he was slightly disappointed.

As he got close enough to the door to see inside, however, the smile came back to his face. The décor inside the venue was attractive, but simple and clean as most cats usually are. There were already dozens of cats mulling around inside and dozens more playing on the grass and trees outside. Yes, this was going to be some party. There was already a good crowd, and the sun wasn't even down yet.

He noticed that the flashing effect of the lights was achieved by having a group of young cats, far too young to attend the party under normal circumstances, covering their assigned lights with a dark or colored cover, which they moved in synch with the music. Caterwaul thought it made for a very impressive visual.

He hadn't yet touched the funds the queen had given him to play with. So tonight, if he needed to, he felt he'd earned the right to indulge himself. He knew these were mostly simple folk, so he didn't expect the royal treatment when it came to food and drink, but he knew he was going to have himself a really good time.

Cueing up took some time. There were a great many cats in front of him in line. As he finally got close to the entrance, he noticed an incredibly cute, soft-looking, chocolate-brown kitty out in front. She was holding some sort of list on a clipboard. Her hair was puffed up and perfumed. Caterwaul thought she smelled fantastic.

"Hi. I am Pudding," she said as Caterwaul approached the door. "What's the name?" The music and noise coming from inside was a little loud so it was hard for Caterwaul to hear.

"I'm sorry," Caterwaul laughed. "Did you just ask me if I wanted some pudding?" he shouted over the music.

"No . . . *I'm* Pudding," she said laughing.

"Well, in that case, I would say the answer is most definitely yes. Pudding is delicious, especially chocolate." He flirtingly extended his paw to her. "I'm Caterwaul."

Flattered, the brown cat batted her eyes at him, but then suddenly became all business. "Mr. Caterwaul, I'm afraid that I don't have your name on my list."

"What?" asked Caterwaul, distracted by the sounds and lights.

"Are you on the invitation list?" she asked.

"No, I am sorry. I don't have a formal invitation. I was told to come out tonight by a friend, a nice foreign gent named Gerhard, whom I met a few days ago. Hopefully you know him? He wears a hat." Caterwaul said loudly over the music, and he motioned awkwardly to the top of his head. "I didn't realize tonight was a private party," he said.

"Oh! Gerhard . . . of course I know Gerhard. He's a riot. We love Gerhard around here, although maybe not so much his breath. Pee yew. His teeth could sure use a good brushing . . . with some of the awful things he'll pop in his mouth. But he's all right. If he told you to come here tonight, then you are most definitely welcome.

"This is a birthday party for my cousin Muse. She is the most beautiful cat in the village. She's not here yet, but I guarantee that you'll know her when you see her," said Pudding.

"Oh, it's a birthday party? No one told me that either. I'm afraid I don't have a gift, but maybe I could show her a magic trick or two. I'm pretty good at those kinds of things," Caterwaul boasted.

"Magic? Oh wonderful!" exclaimed Pudding, jumping up and down. "Muse absolutely loves magic. This is going to be an exciting night. Please make yourself welcome, Mister Caterwaul. We have plenty of food and plenty to drink. We had the milk shipped in all the way from France. Those French cows are the best. Did you know they all speak French over there? It's true . . . I swear. There's just something about the milk from a French cow that makes an extra tasty cocktail, if you ask me."

Pudding walked just inside the door with Caterwaul to show him where the food was. "They tell me that the horse's dovers are just to die for too," she said. "I don't think they're made out of real, horses though, it's just what everyone calls them.

"You really should try the imported caviar too. It's one hundred percent bluegill. As far as I'm concerned, it's nothing but the best for my cousin." She was tremendously excited.

"Am I forgetting anything?" she paused, chewing on her top lip in deep thought. "Oh and yes, we can't forget that there is Pudding . . . That's me," she giggled, winking at Caterwaul and pointing to her chest before going back to the door.

~

The music was excellent, just as Gerhard said it would be. Caterwaul wasn't sure if it was because the musicians had once all been human players, as Gerhard had suggested, or if they were just a bunch of cats imbued with natural talent. One thing was certain: the felines providing the entertainment for this bash really knew what they were doing. They should all be commended for their exceptional ability.

The partygoers seemed quite pleasant, which was very nice seeing how of late he had been dealing almost exclusively with really rotten characters—Coy and Huxley being the exceptions, of course.

It was refreshing for Caterwaul just to be able to relax and enjoy himself for a change. After all, he'd been involved in what seemed like nonstop action since arriving in town. He muttered to himself aloud, "I wonder where the birthday girl is?"

Just then, as if on cue, walking into the old windmill was Muse. Pudding was right. There was no mistaking this animal. She was so beautiful that his heart skipped a beat. His blood started pumping so fast it was as if his ticker was trying to jump out of his chest.

And to make things even better, Caterwaul could see that she was one hundred percent, solid white. What amazing luck—here she was at last. Caterwaul could hardly believe his eyes.

Though Muse was surrounded by an entourage of cats, Pudding went straight up to her and gave her a hug. Taking her cousin by the paw, Pudding led the birthday girl straight to where Caterwaul was sitting on a cushion. Caterwaul jumped to his feet as they got close, because that's what gentlemen do when they are approached by a lady.

"Mr. Caterwaul," said Pudding, "allow me to introduce you to my cousin Muse."

"The pleasure is all mine," said Caterwaul, "I hope you do not find it forward of me to say that you are even more beautiful than I had been led to believe, and they told me you were the most magnificent cat in all the land."

"My, you are a charmer, aren't you?" said Muse with a smile. Her eyes were piercing and blue. "Remind me, cousin, that I need to come back to spend some more time with this one." She glanced around the room and noticed a number of felines that she just had to talk to.

"Until later then, Mr. Caterwaul." She made what appeared to be a curtsey, and he gently bowed his head. As she slid away, she looked back toward where Caterwaul was sitting and smiled.

He grinned back at her and waved his right paw. Muse thought that was cute, and she started to laugh. As he looked at her, her fur appeared to glimmer in the glow of the lighting.

Caterwaul was floored. This Muse was the most beautiful creature he had ever laid eyes on. He stumbled backward for a second, off balance; for he knew he had been struck right through the heart by Cupid's arrow. He took a deep draught of the imported French milk. He couldn't help but notice that Pudding was right. Those French cows indeed made a delicious cocktail.

He addressed his reflection in the milk. *"Il est tre bon monsieur, merci!"*

Caterwaul tried mingling with the other cats, but his eyes kept being drawn toward Muse. Wherever the birthday girl was, she was surrounded by cats. It seemed everyone wanted to be near her. "There is no way this one is getting away," he said to himself aloud. But as the night went on, it didn't look like Muse was going to come back again. She was too occupied with her friends and flatterers.

Then something happened to put the game ball back into Caterwaul's hands. Several cats who were among those rescued from the cage had arrived at the party. As soon as they saw Caterwaul, they started pointing and whispering in the ears of the other cats. Pretty soon, word spread among the guests that there was a genuine hero in their midst.

One by one, they approached Caterwaul and asked him to tell the story of what happened. Then they started coming over to him in groups. Before long, he was surrounded by fawning cats. He listened as cats introduced him as the "heroic cat who risked life and limb to save hundreds of cats from certain death." Every cat wanted to talk to him and shake his paw. The story spread quickly around the windmill in a fire of exaggeration, so that with every telling both the number of cats rescued and the level of peril increased.

Caterwaul couldn't help but notice that Muse started looking toward him more often now. She excused herself from the table where she had been sitting with a group and strolled toward Caterwaul and the throng. When he saw her approaching, he begged the gathering's pardon and promised to reveal to them the entire sordid tale if they would only give him an hour or so alone. Grumbling, the cats agreed, turned, and left him.

"Don't you know it is bad manners to upstage a girl at her own birthday party?" asked Muse only half jokingly. "So . . . they tell me that you're some kind of a hero. What did you do, help get a little old human lady down from a tree?"

"Yes," said Caterwaul playing along. "Did you see me? I was wonderful. You know how it is with those humans . . .

always getting into jams they can't get out of. Curious animals, they are."

She smiled and looked down. "I know how I was when I was human."

"When you were . . . you were human?" he asked her stammering.

"Yes . . . does that surprise you?" she asked him in return.

"Well . . . as a matter of fact, it does actually. I mean you move about so gracefully, I would swear you were a real cat."

"I am a real cat," she said. "I'm just as much a cat as you are or anyone else in this windmill, for that matter."

"I'm sorry . . . That's not what I was trying . . . Oh, you know what I mean. Most newcomers . . . they don't walk right or act right. You know . . . they're not really 'cat-like,'" he explained, "but you don't seem to have any of those problems . . ."

"Adjusting?" she anticipated his next word.

"Yes, that's it exactly."

"Well, that's probably because I actually like being a cat. I prefer it, in fact." She motioned for him to walk with her. "Most of us 'newcomers' as you call us, do not act like cats because we don't want to be cats. We are absolutely terrified by what has happened to us. And how can you blame us? One minute we were living our perfectly uneventful lives as human beings in the village, and then one day, we chanced a look at a mirror—and presto, human no more. Instead we had been mysteriously changed into cats."

She smiled one of those serious half-smiles and looked directly into his eyes. "So it's no wonder that most of us don't make the best cats. Because we're trying with every ounce of our strength and dignity to hold on to what we consider those last shreds of whatever it was that made us human."

"But not you?" asked Caterwaul.

"No . . . not me." She started to move away, hopping up on a handrail. He followed her. "I was never all that good at being human. I much prefer the way my life is now, as Muse the cat." She had a sad look on her face, but it was an inviting one. He moved toward her and put his arm around her.

He knew there was a lot more to her story than she was letting on, but he didn't press her on it. Caterwaul was quite content just to sit there beside her. If she wanted to open up further, later on, he would be glad to listen. At the moment, however, the time for conversation had passed. She tilted her head gently and laid it on his shoulder.

18

The Party Crashers

"So when are you going to show me your magic tricks?" Muse asked him.

"Huh?" asked Caterwaul, who wasn't really listening. He was too busy enjoying himself just sitting there next to this unbelievably beautiful female.

"Magic," she repeated herself. "My cousin Pudding tells me that you can do magic."

"Oh . . . it's nothing more than a few little tricks mainly," he answered, not wanting to reveal that he possessed any depth of skill.

"Do you like magic?" he asked her.

"My father used to do quite a bit of magic for me when I was younger. I must admit that I've always had a soft spot for magicians," she smiled. "What trick do you plan to do?"

He started thinking of a number of quick and easy tricks he might be able to perform to impress her, but he thought none of them was good enough. Then it dawned on him—he might have found a way to kill two birds with one stone.

"I was thinking of sawing you in half," he said jokingly, and she laughed.

"Oh no," she said. "That wouldn't do. How would I get all of the mess out of my beautiful coat?" They were both laughing.

"Now what if I said that I could perform a trick that would get the both of us into Cathoon Castle and have the royal chef make us a grand five-course meal in honor of your birthday?" he asked her with confidence.

"I would say that was impossible," she answered him. "No one goes to Cathoon anymore. No one wants to go to Cathoon. Even when I was just a little girl, nobody wanted to go to that horrible place. The castle is practically empty. The only person who goes anywhere near there now is that awful Queen Druciah—she and her servants, of course.

"I appreciate your sense of humor, but even if you could make that happen, why on earth would I want to go there?"

Caterwaul thought to himself and decided not to continue along those lines for the moment.

"What do you have there in your pack?" Muse asked him. "Is that where you keep your magic? Is it your bag of tricks . . . so to speak?"

Caterwaul smiled and looked into her blue eyes. "My dear, don't you know there are certain questions that should never be asked? A gentleman never asks a lady her age or what she's got in her purse, and a lady never ever asks a magician how the trick is done."

She laughed. "All right . . . you win . . . at least for now, my handsome friend. You can keep your secrets." She started moving toward a staircase leading upstairs and motioned for Caterwaul to follow.

"So, why do you like being a cat so much?" he asked, following her up to a more private spot on the second level.

"Why do you ask? Do you think it strange that someone could prefer to live as a cat rather than as a human being? Okay, I'll tell you. It's because I have never felt so free in all of my life. I wouldn't change back even if I could. Now I can come and go as I please and lie in the sun all day if I want, and I don't have to explain my comings or goings to anyone.

"Life is much simpler now. It's absolutely glorious . . . It's the best thing that's ever happened to me." She rose up on her hind legs and spun around fluidly, like a dancer.

"But what about your family?" Caterwaul asked her. "Don't they miss you? What about your parents and your grandparents?"

"I never knew my grandparents, and both of my parents are gone now. I can remember my mother's face. She was beautiful. One day, when I was just a little girl, a horrible man came and knocked on our door. He said he worked for the queen. Without giving my father any reason, he took my mother away. My father vowed to go after them and to bring mother back, but once he left, I saw neither him nor my mother again.

"So now it's just me . . . and Pudding, of course. She is, or I should say . . . was, quite the dressmaker. You should see her work, it is amazing . . . well, if you were a human girl, you would think so. That's how she supported us.

"Anyway, we lived together in my parents' home. Then one day we were trying on some new dresses she had made, and when we looked into the mirror . . . Poof! We had both been turned into cats. Sure it was strange at first, but I don't think either one of us was entirely happy being human. Whatever sorcery it was that changed us I couldn't tell you, but as it stands, both she and I love being cats."

Rather than get into a discussion about what might have caused the great transformation, Caterwaul cleverly steered the conversation elsewhere.

"Pudding is a rather strange name for a human," noted Caterwaul.

"Oh, that's not her real name, silly," she said. "Her real name is Henrietta-Leigh, but I think we all agree that is rather a large mouthful for a cat to say. Besides, now that she's a cat, we both think she looks much more like a Pudding than a Henrietta. Don't you agree?" She started to giggle.

Caterwaul couldn't argue with Muse's logic there. He started to laugh. "You know it really does suit her." They were now both roaring.

Just then there was a commotion at the door. The music stopped suddenly, and everyone in the old windmill looked in the direction of the entrance to see just what was going on.

"Oh no . . . It's Gerhard!" Caterwaul shouted.

Limping through the doorway, barely supported by two other cats, was Gerhard. He looked as if he had just been through a war. He was bleeding from any number of cuts and deep scratches. His pale gray fur had been yanked out of his flesh in tufts, so that his skin was bare and raw in many places. His legs were wobbly and he could not support his weight without help. He looked as though he had been tortured for a long time. His trademark hat was nowhere to be seen.

Caterwaul could see Pudding standing near the beaten cat. She was in a state of near panic. Her eyes darted wildly about the room looking for help. His eyes locked with hers, and he saw her mouth the words "help me." Immediately he jumped from his place on the second level toward the spot where the beaten Gerhard had been gently set down.

Landing spryly on the ground, Caterwaul ran to his friend. "Gerhard, what happened?" he asked.

Two other cats came running up at that point. The first carried a wet towel and the second a small container of water. They obviously knew him and were his friends. Gerhard took a deep drink of the water and started gasping as the first cat wiped the blood from his cut up face.

"Caterwaul . . . I . . . I'm . . . I'm so sorry," he said sputtering. "It was the Felinos." He was choking and sputtering as he gulped the air. Caterwaul suspected that he might have cracked ribs, or worse a punctured lung. The gangsters obviously had worked him over thoroughly.

"They know you're here, mate." He was crying ashamedly. "I gave you up. They did things to me, horrible things. I had to. I'm so . . . so sorry mate. They're coming for you. They'll be here soon."

In the back of the ground floor of the windmill, there was a special room that had been lined with rugs and padded with cushions. There were cushions enough for at least ten cats to rest on comfortably or to sleep off any ill effects which may have developed from their drinking too much of the imported French cows' milk.

Caterwaul motioned for Pudding to help him get the resting cats up. "Everyone get out of the back area now! Move it! Call the purramedics; we have a cat down!" he shouted.

Once Gerhard had been safely moved to the padded area, Caterwaul asked the wounded tom to tell him exactly what had happened to him. Gerhard told him that he had gone to see Lucius Jr. to sell him information about the queen's secret policeman.

The injured feline explained that just the casual mention of Caterwaul's name enraged the feline underboss so much that he ordered his men to seize him by the forepaws and beat him mercilessly. Caterwaul was worried. He looked behind and noticed that Muse had crept up beside him. She looked frightened. She knew who Lucius Felino Jr. was, and she knew he was one dangerous kitty.

"We've got to get out of here," said Muse.

"I can't just leave him," snapped Caterwaul. "Friends don't leave friends when there's trouble."

"But he said that the Felinos are coming," cried Muse. "We can't be here when they get here. If they did all this to

Gerhard, they'll kill you."

The cat who had been wiping clean Gerhard's wounds spoke, "Go . . . Get away. My brother and I will look after him. And there are others here who are friends of Gerhard. Trust me. My name is Juan. Nothing more will happen to him. Not if we can help it.

"My brother Feliz and I have been friends with Gerhard since he first arrived in the village. We will not let anything else happen to him." Caterwaul glanced at Feliz. He was a pretty small cat. Juan was not a whole lot bigger, but both animals looked strong and healthy. Still, he wondered how these two average-looking cats would manage to hold off the Felinos' muscle.

As if he knew what Caterwaul was thinking, Feliz popped his claws out. Caterwaul couldn't believe what he was seeing. His claws were enormous. They looked like the talons of an animal twice his size, and as far as he could tell, they were sharp as daggers. They were the cultivated weapons of an animal that knew how to handle himself in a fight. Feliz flashed a big old toothy grin at Caterwaul and nodded confidently, letting him know Gerhard was in good hands.

"Come on Muse, let's move," said Caterwaul.

The black cat and Muse started to break toward the doorway. Just then, Pudding came running in, flailing her front paws that they should stop. "Caterwaul no! You can't go out that way . . . It's too late," she screamed. "The Felinos . . . They're already here!"

19

Very Bad Kitties

Pudding's words ricocheted around the stone windmill like six-pound cannonballs that had been fired inside.

Suddenly the cats, who had become quiet at the sight of Gerhard, all went into a panic. They scrambled for whichever exit they could find.

Most of the cats tried to get out through the main exit and were stopped dead in their tracks and driven back inside by the gangsters. A few who had jumped from open windows appeared to have escaped, but the majority of the cats, including most of the recently transformed, just froze or ran aimlessly into one another. Many were knocked over onto their backs, which is unusual when dealing with such surefooted animals as cats.

Even from several yards inside the old windmill, Caterwaul could see that she was right. There would be no running away. The outfit had definitely come, and they had come in force. This time it was a lot more than just Lucius Jr. and two trained gorillas. There were a lot of them out there, and they were closing in to surround the old windmill. Caterwaul could count at least eight just in his field of vision.

"Is there a back way out of here?" Caterwaul asked.

"Yes, but there are probably at least three of them watching it by now," Pudding answered him. "I wouldn't risk trying it."

Caterwaul looked back at Muse. She was practically frozen

with fear. He knew if he was going to be able to escape this trap, it would be impossible dragging a terrified cat behind him. He immediately thought of Juan and Feliz.

Staring with utmost seriousness into Pudding's eyes he said, "Take your cousin to the back of the windmill where Gerhard is. Juan and his brother are there. They will protect you. Go now!" he ordered.

Muse was shaking with fear. She looked up at Caterwaul with her big blue eyes and stammered, "Please . . . don't go. Don't leave me here."

"I don't want to! Muse, I swear it! But the Felinos are after me. If I stay here or if I try to take you with me, we're both going to be caught. You saw what they did to Gerhard. I beat up Lucius Jr. I embarrassed him in front of his family. Can you imagine what they plan to do to me? And they will torture you, too, just for being with me. I won't have that. I like you, Muse. I like you a lot, and I won't have you hurt because of me.

"Pudding . . . Get yourselves to safety, now!"

With only a split second's hesitation, Pudding grabbed Muse by the forepaw and dashed with fear toward the sanctuary of the cushioned room.

Caterwaul didn't know what to do next. There were Felinos inside the building now, as well as out. The trapped partygoers were scared and showing no signs they were willing to resist. Caterwaul tore wildly up the stairs to the second and then to the third level. There, a number of cats were trying to hide, either by standing motionless or hiding under clumps of hay, fabric, or other sources of cover. Caterwaul tripped over one of the hidden cats who instinctively shot his paw out at him with claws out.

The cat struck him sharply in the left hind leg, and Caterwaul fell over screaming.

"Sorry, man," whispered the cat from under the hay, which

concealed him. "I didn't mean it. You stepped on me, and I just reacted. Instinct, you know?"

Caterwaul hoped that his outcry did not give him away. He was wrong. Looking down from his position high above the ground, he could see Lucius Jr. pointing up at him and motioning for his men to pursue. Jr. was looking confident today. He had at least twelve soldiers with him inside the windmill. There were probably an equal number stationed outside waiting.

Saliva flew from Lucius' mouth as he barked orders to his men. His face was marked by a big, stupid grin and his fat belly shook as he watched the terrified Caterwaul trying to escape.

Everything about this Felino underboss repulsed him. But there was one thing about his appearance in the windmill that particularly angered Caterwaul. There, sitting on the top of Lucius Jr.'s enormously grotesque head, held in place only by the use of a strap, was Gerhard's sailor's cap.

Caterwaul was shaking as he climbed, terrified and angry at the same time. He thought he was done for. Surely the Felinos would get him and do all sorts of terrible things to him. And to think he had gotten so close. Well, at least they wouldn't hurt his beautiful Muse now.

~

Pudding pulled Muse back into the farthest and darkest corner of the cushioned room, trying to get her cousin out of sight.

"Caterwaul said that you'd keep us safe," she whispered to the guardian brothers. Juan nodded that he understood and took up a defensive position at the front and left of Gerhard. At the same time, Feliz took up a similar one on the right.

The smaller brother was smiling as he tapped his oversized claws on the stone floor like a piano player practicing his scales. He had incredible dexterity and could snap his claws in or out with blinding speed. Pudding imagined the amount of damage he was capable of inflicting with those razors. Feliz was itching for a good scrap.

Juan scanned the room for pillows with rope tassels on them. He saw three. "Grab those cushions with the ropes attached to them and bring them here," he spoke quietly to the frightened Pudding. She was scared, but she moved forward to do what he asked. Muse squeezed Pudding's paw as if to beg her not to move; she was trying desperately not to cry.

"I'll be right back," Pudding whispered to her cousin. "Don't worry; I'm right here with you. I'm not going anywhere, I promise." Once she had gathered the three pillows with the tassels, Juan instructed her to make a slit in the center of the fabric covering each. She then loaded them with four good-sized rocks and slid them down into the corner opposite the tassel.

"Can you lift them?" asked Juan. "The cushions . . . Can you still lift them?"

"Yes . . . I think so," said Pudding.

"Good. Now here is what I want you to do," he leaned forward and whispered something in her ear.

~

"Hey, tough guy," shouted Lucius Felino Jr. to the fleeing Caterwaul. "Where do you think you're going, tough guy? The family's here, and everyone wants to meet you." He let out a huge, satisfied laugh. "You're not so tough now, are you?"

"Why don't you crawl on back down here now, so as I can make the introductions . . . you know . . . all formal and proper-like. After all, just because we may be animals doesn't mean that we gotta act like animals, if you catch my drift." He was laughing hysterically at his own weak joke.

Caterwaul heard all of this, but kept moving. He knew that

Lucius Jr. was only taunting him. He knew they would torture him mercilessly if they caught him. More than likely, he would be killed. He remembered the powder he had taken from the sycamore seedpods. Turning swiftly he removed his pack. The pursuing Felinos were still quite a ways off.

He grabbed the piece of folded up paper he had placed the seeds in and opened it. He had more than enough for one use, but then it would be gone. It was one and done, he thought. Oh well, now was as good a time as ever.

He was now positioned on a narrow wooden ledge between the fourth and fifth level of the windmill. He pressed his body close to the wall hoping that the Felinos would not see him hiding above them when they reached level four.

About a minute later, they were right below him. There were three of them, and they appeared confused. Their sense of smell indicated that they were close, but they did not know exactly where their quarry was. The one who appeared to be the leader placed his paws on the handrail and raised himself up to signal to his boss below that they had lost him. He shrugged his shoulders.

"Trust me, he's up there!" shouted Lucius Jr. "Find him. He can't have just disappeared."

Caterwaul smiled. As a matter of fact, he *could* disappear. But that was an ability he dared not use right now. Use of that particular incantation, like most of his more powerful ones, drained a terrible amount of energy from him. If he were to use the spell, he would be useless if they later found him and it came to blows. Besides, he didn't dare do anything that might leave Muse unprotected.

~

Two of the Felino bruisers came into view near the cushioned room. Muse saw them, and it looked like she was about to explode with fright. She started whimpering for her cousin and pointing toward the big, muscular cats. Pudding put her finger to her mouth to quiet her cousin, but it was a lot to ask of the terrified cat.

"I see Gerhard over there. Lying on those cushions," said one of the Felinos to his buddy. "It looks like he's pretty much out of action from the beating we gave him earlier. I don't think he'll present any problems, but go tell the boss that he's here anyway."

While the second thug turned and ran back to where Lucius Jr. was, the first one approached the prone Gerhard slowly. Gerhard was unconscious and his breathing was erratic. The Felino bruiser soon stood directly over his near-lifeless body. The gray foreigner had been seriously hurt. He was only inches from the great and final finish line marking the end of his life.

How easy it would be to snuff out that life, thought the bruiser. He popped out his index claw and held it precariously close to Gerhard's throat. All it would take is one swipe, he thought.

Suddenly the large Felino's eyes rolled back in his head and he went limp. As he fell backward, he tried to stop his fall by grabbing at anything he could. He found nothing, and he toppled. As he looked up, the last thing he saw before blackness was the wide-smiling Feliz shaking a fur-covered paw at him.

~

Caterwaul waited until all three of the Felinos chasing him were bunched closely together, and then he sprung toward them. As he leaped, he opened the folded paper containing the "itchy powder" from the sycamore pods. The dusty fibers spread out, covering the three Felino thugs below him. As he landed, he took off in the direction of the fifth level.

"There he is. Grab him," shouted the leader. The three soldier cats barely made it as far as the stairs up to the next landing before they started itching uncontrollably. "What in the world?!" the lead cat shouted as he doubled over and began scratching himself.

All three of the Felino soldiers were affected by the seed fibers. They gnawed and pawed and swiped at their flesh with their open claws, tearing long red gashes in their skin. It was as if all three of them had fallen simultaneously into a bucketful of fleas. The cries they let out were horrible. Everyone on the ground wondered what awful thing was happening on the fourth level. Suddenly it became clear as one of the incapacitated felines fell flailing to the ground below. He landed on one of his fellow ruffians with a splat.

Then a second cat came tumbling through the air. This time the cat seemed so preoccupied with something on his skin that he had no idea that he was hurtling toward the ground. This time those on the ground were sensible enough to move out of the way, and the cat landed hard. He shrieked in agony, but still he didn't stop scratching his itchy skin.

"Please don't throw me over," the leader of the three cats pleaded. "I promise you I'll go away . . . you'll never ever see me again."

Caterwaul wasn't fazed. Grabbing the Felino by his fancy collar, he dragged him to the edge of the platform. Looking fiercely at the squirming cat beneath him, Caterwaul snarled, "This is for Gerhard," and kicked him over the edge. The tomcat screamed, twisting in terror as he fell and landed on his back below.

Now furiously defiant, Caterwaul jumped up onto the top of the handrail and shouted down to Lucius Jr. "Is that all you got, you fat sack of sandbox droppings?"

On the ground below, Lucius Felino Jr. roared. He was foaming at the mouth now and copious amounts of thick, white drool flew out of it in all directions. "I want him dead! Now!" He screamed to his remaining men. "You hear me?"

~

Noticing that one of their companions had not returned from his investigation of the unconscious Gerhard, two Felino soldiers went looking for him. As they neared the incapacitated cat, Juan and Feliz sprang at them from the shadows. The cats appeared to be evenly matched, though the fight was fierce. For a while it looked like Feliz might have the advantage over his opponent, but then looks often deceive.

The much larger Felino soldier was tough as they come, and he was more than able to withstand the swipes of even Feliz's oversized claws. Feliz swung his paws at him repeatedly, but still the Felino kept coming. Finally the big cat was able to knock Feliz over onto his back. It was over. Feliz could feel the larger cat's paws pressing tightly against his throat as he lost consciousness.

Juan was holding up well against his opponent, but now that Feliz was out of the fight, he knew his time was short. There was no way he could take on both his man and the cat that had just KO'd his brother. Especially since Feliz was acknowledged by most of Harsizzle as the better fighter of the two.

Frightened, Juan flailed out, wildly throwing his paws out in all directions at the same time. He was starting to panic. They had him in a vulnerable position with his back up against one of the pillars separating the cushion room from the rest of the old windmill. They moved toward him from two directions, making sure that he could not get away. At that moment, something large and heavy connected with the face of one of the Felino cats. He cried out for an instant before falling over. The gangster was knocked out cold.

The remaining Felino soldier spun around to see who or what it was that had just crushed his companion's face. It was Pudding, and she was angry. In her hands she held one of the ropes, which were attached to one of the tasseled pillows. With the rocks inside the pillow it was very heavy, and it was all she could do to keep her balance as she spun it around her body. Following through, she delivered a ferocious uppercut with the pillow, hitting the second thug so hard in his soft belly that it literally lifted the cat off his feet.

She was wild-eyed and full of fury, snarling as she held on tightly to the rope tassel. Juan moved in to calm her down. Her nostrils flared, and she looked back at him with crazed eyes. She was trembling from the sudden adrenaline rush. It looked for a moment like she might lash out at her protector. Then suddenly she was back in control. Sanity returned to the young cat's eyes.

Pudding was starting to tear up. Never in a million years would she have thought she'd have to do what she did that night. Looking back and seeing that her cousin was still safe, she dropped the pillow and sank to the ground weeping.

Juan motioned to Muse to come over and together the two of them wrapped their arms tightly around a very scared, very brave, chocolate-colored kitty, who just might have saved all of their lives.

20

What Goes Around

T here were now three more Felino soldiers on his tail. "Bring 'em on," thought Caterwaul out loud, "I'll take out the whole family . . . every last rotten one of them."

He looked around for his pack, but it wasn't where he thought it was. Then he remembered he'd left it hanging on a nail above the ledge between the fourth and fifth levels. He was now on the sixth level. To get to it, he would have to give up some ground and head toward his enemies.

But did he even have time to go back for it? *Probably not*, he thought. It was too dangerous, not worth the risk. Plus, these new pursuers were moving up the stairs between levels at a good clip, much faster than the first trio.

His rush of adrenaline was subsiding, and suddenly he was reminded of the pain in his leg from when he had stepped on the hidden cat. Reflexively his paw flew to the spot where the cat had tagged him. It was still bleeding slowly, and there was a piece of fur-covered skin hanging loose from his wound.

"Owwwwww!" he shouted, as everyone does when they first discover they have been cut. "This is going to slow me down."

He then realized there might be a way for him to use his injury to his advantage. At the end of the sixth level, there was a small window. Through it, he could see one of the wooden blades of the windmill. It wasn't moving.

The windmill was the kind often used to pump water for irrigation. It had been turned off before the event. The party planners didn't want to leave it running for fear that it might somehow stop and cause a sudden swell of water. He understood this perfectly because he knew how most cats felt about large amounts of water.

He yanked the hanging bit of skin and hair sharply away from his body. He could hear a loud tear as a clump of his leg came loose in his paw. Caterwaul wanted to scream, but he didn't dare. Instead he moved methodically toward the window, making sure to smear the blood from his piece of now-unattached flesh, leaving a trail on the boards going up to the window. He then dropped the clump of skin out the window. It bounced a couple of times on the outside of the windmill before landing silently in the weeds below. He then backed away quietly and hid behind a red canvas tarp.

By the time the three Felinos had reached the sixth level, they were out of steam. The one in the lead position was sucking in air like he had just run a marathon. Between his loud deep breaths, he managed to get out two words, "Find him."

The other two cats spread out to search the level, but none of the three cats were in any shape to do it right. Meanwhile, the first cat had discovered the trail of blood and was following it toward the open window.

He was still gasping when he got up to it, and he put his paws up on the sill for a better look. He could see the signs of blood on the outside wall and assumed, as Caterwaul had hoped he would, that his prey was no longer inside the windmill.

Turning back to his companions, he called, "He's gone. He went out this window. Probably long gone by now." He was still breathing heavily when he told the others to head back down to inform Lucius Jr.

~

Juan was trying to get Feliz to his feet. He had been out cold for nearly half an hour before any sign of consciousness returned to him. He was gagging and wheezing. The Felino that choked him was obviously out to hurt him permanently.

"I can walk," the smaller brother said to the other. Then he noticed the two Felinos lying in a lump on the floor. "What in the world happened to them?"

"Pudding happened to them!" exclaimed the brown female proudly.

"Huh?" Feliz asked, confused. "What do you mean?"

Juan laughed and put his paw over his still-weak brother's shoulder for support. "Leez, do you remember the old blackjack maneuver we used to pull on the Umbertos back when we lived in Sullins?"

"You mean back when we were stupid kids? How could I ever forget? You were always getting us into trouble." He was laughing. "Man, I remember when that big cat Mo from down the street kicked the stuffing out of you and tore your face up."

Feliz continued laughing until it was clear that Juan preferred not to take this stroll down memory lane any further than he had to. Feliz got serious. "Yes, I remember," he said matter-of-factly.

"Well, tonight we turned the damage level up a few extra notches." Juan pointed to the pillow with the rocks inside, which Pudding had used to lay out the two Felinos. "Man, you should have seen her. She was fearless."

"I would hardly say I was fearless, Juan," replied Pudding. "I was scared to death. But after you went down, Feliz, I just went berserk. There were two of them against Juan. I just wanted to help even the odds."

She looked at Muse. The white cat was at last starting to

calm down. Her breathing was returning to normal, and other signs of shock were dissipating. "I hope that Caterwaul got away," she said, concerned.

~

The Felino who had been leading the second trio of mobsters turned back to the window and leaned out. It looked like he was about to call to one of his family members outside the windmill to tell him that Caterwaul was on the loose below. As the thug cat leaned forward a little more to try and spot one of his "fellas," Caterwaul attacked. Propelling himself forward with all of his weight, he caught the Felino in the back with his front right shoulder, knocking him through the window.

Though he was still slightly winded, the Felino righted himself in mid-fall, twisting around to avoid the windmill panels, and hit the ground on all fours. Unfortunately for him, the window was still six floors up, more than enough to injure even the most acrobatic of cats—and this big Felino was no acrobat. He managed to land on his feet, but the force with which he hit the ground undoubtedly broke at least one of his legs. He staggered forward a few steps and fell over on his side, calling out in pain.

"Man . . . that had to hurt," said Caterwaul squeezing his eyes together and making his face really small. He suddenly realized how high up he actually was.

Turning back inside, he started moving toward the stairway leading down to the fifth level. After all, he knew the other two cats were heading downstairs to tell Lucius Jr. the bad news about Caterwaul's supposed escape. Only when he got close to the steps did Caterwaul realize only one of the two cats had followed orders. The other one was just sitting on his haunches with a dopey expression, enjoying what was left of a partially mummified mouse. The dry and cracking tail of the mouse protruded from his mouth as he stared up at Caterwaul with surprise and alarm in his eyes.

"Oops," said Caterwaul as he jumped backward.

The Felino spit the remains of his impromptu dinner on the floor and scrambled to his feet. Like most of Lucius' soldiers, he was a large, muscular tom. He was colored with light orange stripes. Caterwaul thought the cat looked like he might be Bugsy's stripy brother. He had that same stupid look on his face.

Since he no longer had his pack with him and was injured, Caterwaul didn't think much of his chances in a fight with this bruiser. The Felino was much bigger than Caterwaul and not hampered by a gammy leg. Caterwaul believed his best option was to run. Pivoting in an about-face, he fled back toward the window again.

"Why did it have to be so high up?" Caterwaul asked himself as he climbed up on the window ledge. One look back revealed his pursuer was closing in, so he closed his eyes and leaped out of the window and onto one of the moving wind panels. Surprisingly, he was able to get his footing quickly. The blade of the windmill had many small crevices he could sink his claws into to gain purchase.

Within seconds, he was in a good position to look back to the window. He noticed the bigger cat was already on the windowsill, hissing and ready to pounce on Caterwaul.

~

"Let's get out of here," said Pudding. There was a lot of commotion, and she figured it was only a matter of time before someone discovered what she had done to the two Felino soldiers. Feliz and Juan grabbed the limp bodies of the unconscious gangsters and dragged them toward the back of the cushion room. They completely covered both cats with pillows to hide them before returning to where the females stood.

Gerhard was now conscious, but in no condition to move,

much less try to make a break for it. "Leave me," he said. "Move me back into the other corner and cover me like you did those two leg-breakers," he said. "I'll try to stay quiet enough so that no one will notice me."

The brothers carried Gerhard to the far corner, hiding him beneath the cushions, as he had requested. Still they were reluctant to leave their good friend unattended.

"Go on now, fellas. You got ladies need protecting," said the injured cat. His head was all that remained uncovered. "Don't worry about me, mates. I can take care of myself. You know this. So just go on and get those females to safety." As they started moving back to the girls, they heard him talking to himself: "Now where the blazes did I leave my hat?"

Gerhard watched as his protectors headed out. He saw Muse step fully out into the light and noticed she had pure-white fur. "Wait 'til Caterwaul gets a load of her," he snickered aloud to himself. Smiling and shaking his head, he continued his one-sided conversation. "Very pretty . . . But she's just a bit too skinny for me. I like 'em with a lot more meat on their bones." He ducked his head beneath the cushions and disappeared from sight.

"So which is the best way out?" Juan asked, turning toward Pudding. "I mean, so we can best slip away unnoticed."

"Well, the front door is out, and the basement is sealed off. I suppose that the best route would be to see if the back door has opened up. The four cats tried to move as fast and silently as possible to where the rear exit was. They were in luck. It appeared to be clear.

"Come on. The door is unguarded," purred Juan. He grabbed Pudding by the paw and pulled her forward. Pudding did the same to Muse, while Feliz guarded their rear.

Once all four cats had safely crossed the threshold to the outside, Pudding let out a sigh of relief. "We made it," she said excitedly, grabbing Juan's paw tightly in hers. "We're free." Just then, there was a sound like a whip and the trap sprung. The four cats were pulled immediately skyward. They were all four caught in a large rope net.

From behind a tree stepped a medium sized gray-and-black stripy. He was chewing on a stem of long grass. Even with the lack of light the trapped cats could see that both his face and most of his upper body were covered in scars.

"Good evening ladies and gents," said the stripy cat arrogantly. "Allow me to introlucidate myself. My name is Meyer."

~

Caterwaul snarled back at the Felino on the ledge, challenging him to follow. It was true that the gangster cat was a lot larger than he was, but Caterwaul was betting the big animal would be lacking when it came to agility and possibly courage too.

When the Felino hesitated to jump after him, Caterwaul knew he was right. The mob soldier continued to hiss, spit, and paw threateningly in his direction, but it was all a smoke screen. It was obvious that the big cat was afraid to follow him. Soon it became apparent to the Felino that he wasn't fooling anyone with his faux ferocity. He then realized he could still call for help.

There were a number of family members outside the old windmill. When they heard one of their own calling out, they all looked up and saw what he was shouting about. Caterwaul, the reason they all had come here, was trapped on one of the windmill blades.

One of the grounded soldiers ran inside and within seconds he emerged with his capo. Lucius Felino Jr. smiled, giggling excitedly as he looked up to where his enemy was trapped on the blade above him. Since he now had Caterwaul cornered, Lucius Jr. lost interest in keeping those remaining party guests prisoner. As soon as he called his remaining men outside, the frightened guests bolted in all directions.

"How long do you actually think you can evade me by staying up on that windmill blade?" Lucius Jr. asked, laughing so loudly it could almost be called a howl. "It's only a matter of time, my elusive friend, before you tire and fall or one of my men climbs up there and grabs you." Caterwaul held on for dear life. He knew he was caught, but he wasn't going to give up easily.

"What will I do with you once I have you? Hmmm? You know I'm thinking that I might eat you." About a dozen eyes locked on Jr. in disbelief. Even his men were sickened by the thought. The fat kitten continued as his enormous belly rumbled. "I've never eaten another cat before. I wonder what it tastes like. It probably tastes like chicken. Isn't that what they say? Everything strange and new tastes just like chicken?" He paused, then stared up at his quarry with an evil glare.

"You want to know something Caterwaul?" he shouted up at the windmill blade. "I'm quite fond of chicken. It's delicious." He turned to one of his men. "Get inside and find the locking mechanism that keeps those blades in place. I want you to release it. Let's see how long our furry black friend can stay balanced on that thing if it's moving."

~

Feliz unsheathed his massive claws and prepared to cut them free of the net. He looked around above him searching for the weak spot to slash.

"Oh, I wouldn't do that if I were you. You might fall on your head and break your neck, or worse . . . you might end up seriously injuring one of your lovely lady friends." Meyer rolled the stem of grass in his lips from one side of his mouth to the other. Feliz kept his claws drawn, and he snarled defiantly at his captor. Meyer was impressed by the set of daggers Feliz had jutting from his paws.

"Oh, put those horrible things away before you hurt yourself." He grinned and stared straight into Feliz's eyes.

"You want down? Put away those pig stickers, and I just might grant you your wish." Feliz hesitated, and Meyer, who was losing patience, barked at him. "You heard me cat. I said claws, away . . . now!"

Feliz retracted his claws into his paws.

"Good," said Meyer, "now we understand each other." The stripy gangster whistled, and five more Felinos stepped into view. "Just so you don't get any wild ideas," he said. "Let 'em down Bugsy and not too gently."

It was only then that the trapped cats saw they were not suspended in the air by any device, but by one large and extremely powerful yellow cat. As they looked out from the net, they could see him clearly. He wasn't even breaking a sweat. He held four fully grown felines aloft in a net and did it with ease. It was like their weight was nothing to this big yellow cat.

Bugsy let go of the rope, and the net fell to the ground. The cats landed with a thud. Feliz had been suspended upside down, so he landed on his back between his shoulder blades. He was glad that he had put away his claws.

The Felinos cleared away the net, and the four freed cats clambered to their feet. "Now I don't want no funny stuff, you two," said Meyer addressing Feliz and Juan. "I hear you can fight. I advise you not to get any ideas. If you start acting crazy, Bugsy here will rip you apart.

"And you . . . with that fine set of Christmas cutlery up your sleeve," he was talking directly to Feliz now. "You might think that because you and me are about the same size you can take me on. Trust me you can't. You make one move toward me, and I'll kill ya quick. There's lotsa cats buried in the dirt 'round here that was bigger, stronger, faster, and a lot scarier than you are, cupcake. I put 'em there . . ." he paused for a moment.

"I want you to look at me closely. Don't be scared . . . I know I'm a beauty," he said sarcastically. "Really take a good look at me. No cat gets a face like this without being in a whole lotta fights. And as pretty as I am . . . you should see the other guys. So play it cool and these guys won't have to bury any bodies tonight."

He took two steps toward where Feliz was standing. "Oh yeah, and there's one more thing, cupcake. You ain't the only one here that's carrying a conceited weapon." He smiled widely, drawing back his gums to reveal an enormous set of fangs. "They say I'm a throwback to my prehysterical ancestors. You ever hear of a saber tooth tiger, cupcake?" He turned to address the girls.

"Now regardless to you, young ladies, I've been watchin' botha you for a while now," he said. "I must say, my little brown friend, you impressed the heck outta me the way you took out Zero and Carmine." He started laughing loudly, "Those two are gonna be useless for weeks. Rocks in a pillow . . . that's awesome. Gonna have to remember that one. Have to keep an extra close eye on you too.

"Which leads me to you gorgeous," he said, staring directly at Muse. "You sure are a looker. You're my kinda gal. I would keep you all for myself if only my boss didn't have plans for you. He's got this scenario working, and you, my dear, get to play a starring role."

Muse looked back at him horrified. She could hardly bear to look at his mangled features. This cat was frightening.

"You didn't know I was watching you the whole time, did you?" he asked her. You didn't know that I was there hiding in the background, just watching as you and him held hands and you laid your head on his furry shoulder all romantic-like." He flashed his enormous teeth at her, and she jumped back.

"My boss is absolutely dying to meet you, Muse. You're gonna be the bait that draws Caterwaul right to us."

21

The Crooner

aterwaul held on tightly as the windmill blades began to move. Lucius Jr. was determined to bring him down from his high perch by whatever means necessary. As the blade started dipping toward the ground, Caterwaul inched his way toward the center and leaped across to the opposite one that was rising. As the new blade rose it came precariously close to the Felino on the windowsill. Caterwaul had to duck and slip down toward the hub to avoid being raked by his claws.

This went on for a good twenty minutes. Lucius Jr. screamed in frustration from the ground below. Twice he ordered his cats to climb up the stones covering the outside of the windmill, and both times, they fell back to earth after trying to grab onto one of the blades. The cats tried to knock him off by throwing stones at him, but Caterwaul either nimbly dodged them or, if they hit him, they weren't enough to make him let go. He was hanging on for his very life.

Then the worst thing Caterwaul could imagine happened. A large group of Felinos emerged from inside the windmill and with them, their collars chained together, were Pudding, Juan, and Feliz. His heart sank. His friends were nicked. Undoubtedly the underboss was going to use them as bargaining chips. He didn't know what to do.

At least they didn't have Muse, he thought. Maybe she had been able to slip away with the other cats when Jr. went outside. At least that was what he hoped had happened. But hope faded quickly as he saw Meyer on the ground below walking toward his employer. Even from high up he knew it was Meyer. That jigsaw puzzle face of his was unmistakable. He held in his paw a rope noose, the business end of which was around the throat of a beautiful white cat, Muse.

They had her too. Bugsy walked behind Muse, as if to challenge anyone to try to free her. It was clear to Caterwaul he hadn't really gotten the whole "Bugsy picture" that day out in the tall grass. The yellow cat was a monster. He had the right job as muscle for the Felinos. In fact, he had muscles on top of the muscles he took to work. Caterwaul realized it was only pure luck and his magical powder that had gotten him through that first encounter. He did not relish a rematch, especially not with his pack inaccessible, hanging in the old windmill.

Lucius Jr. yelled up at him. "Hey, Mr. Fancypants, time to knock off the hijinks." He took the rope from Meyer and tugged it, causing the noose to tighten slightly around Muse's throat. "You're pretty good with the jumping around all willy nilly. I might put you on the road in the circus. That is, if I wasn't going to kill ya."

Caterwaul felt the windmill panels slow and then stop. One of the gangsters must have restored the braking mechanism. He turned around and dug his claws deep into the gaps in the blade. This gave him the best position possible to see what was going on below and avoid being knocked to the ground.

"It's time for you and me to make a deal," the mob boss hissed.

"If you hurt Muse or any of my friends, Jr., I swear I will tear you apart," Caterwaul shouted back.

Lucius Jr. cackled at the thought. "Big talk, coming from a cat who won't even come down here to face me. I tell you what . . . This is how it's going to go. You are going to come down from there right now. If you try to stall, I will turn one of your friends over to Meyer and Bugsy. In fact, I have a good idea which one I'm going to give them first." He tugged on the rope again, and Muse gasped.

"You have ten seconds . . . the clock is ticking. Tick tock tick tock." On every tock, he jerked the noose a little tighter.

From his place up on the windmill, Caterwaul shook nervously. "All right, Jr., you win. Just please don't hurt her," he implored the Felino below. "I'm coming down right now."

Just to make clear that he was the one in charge, Lucius Jr. gave one more tug on the rope tightening the noose a little more. "Quit wasting my time," he shouted, "and get your tail down here."

Caterwaul was beaten. He had no choice. If he didn't surrender himself to this insane cat, his friends would be seriously hurt. He scrambled down the windmill blades and jumped to the ground.

"Okay, I'm here. Now let my friends go." Two family members immediately grabbed him by his front legs.

Lucius Jr. grinned. "Oh no . . . not just yet. They are going to stand here and watch what I'm going to do to you."

Muse was crying. "I'm so sorry, Caterwaul," she whimpered, "for getting you caught like this."

"It's not your fault, Muse, it's mine. I should have taken care of this bully the first time we met."

"Yeah, but you didn't," snapped Jr. "And now I am gonna get riddaya for good." With every word, spray flew from his mouth. He was quaking with excitement. Whenever Lucius Jr. became extra excited, the drool came. Right now he was positively raving, and the saliva poured like a waterfall from the corners of his open mouth.

"Bugsy," he howled, "you got dibs."

Bugsy lumbered forward smiling. "I'm gonna hurt you now." He did not even draw his claws. This was going to be an old-fashion beat down. Bugsy drew back and slammed Caterwaul in his exposed chest with an open paw. The other Felinos let go because they wanted to watch Bugsy dismantle him one blow at a time.

Caterwaul, the wind knocked out of him, couldn't even muster the energy to defend himself. The enormous mobster grabbed him under the front legs and flung him, end over end, against a tree.

"This is way too easy," said Lucius Jr. "Come on now, Caterwaul. This isn't what I expected from the guy who just flattened three of my best guys. Fight back, you coward."

"Actually, it was four, you miserable waste of meat, but who's counting." Caterwaul remained defiant. He realized he was getting creamed, but he was not going to give his foe any satisfaction by acknowledging it. Pushing himself up onto his feet, he sprang toward the big yellow cat. Bugsy stepped aside, grabbed him by his neck skin, and flipped him over like a kitten's plaything.

"I know what might make you fight better," spewed the underboss. "Hey Meyer . . . You always had a thing for white cats. Take her, my gift to you, for your years of loyal service to the Felino family."

He handed the rope to his lieutenant. Meyer flashed his saber teeth and started leading Muse back inside the windmill. She was horrified. But if she tried to pull away, the noose drew tighter about her throat.

"If he so much as touches her, Felino, I will end you. I will end every last one of you," Caterwaul said, enraged.

"Merely hot air, my friend," said the corpulent cat. "Look at yourself. You can't get past Bugsy. You don't have the stuff to beat even one of my crew. You'd need an army to beat us all."

Then from out of nowhere, Caterwaul heard singing. It was beautiful.

"Foolish cats rush in, where kittens fear to tread . . . "

Lucius Jr. lost his train of thought. Suddenly everybody stopped what they were doing to listen to the melodious voice.

At that moment, a white cat appeared on the ridge overlooking the fray. It was Frankie, the white male that Caterwaul rescued from Warwick Vane Bezel III. And he brought company. It was he who sang. Surrounding the crooner on both sides, there were cats—and lots of them. Caterwaul estimated there were at least fifteen, maybe even twenty cats with him. They all remained silent and motionless as the crooner sang the rest of the verse.

From his place on the ridge Frankie called to the Felinos below. "Did I hear somebody mention an army? Because gentlemen, the kitty cavalry has arrived."

Frankie signaled for his cats to attack. They had the mobsters outnumbered three to one. But the Felinos were big cats and used to fighting, so the odds were pretty even. Still, Frankie brought some tough customers with him. The outcome was in no way certain.

The sudden melee drew the attention of the Felinos who had been assigned to watch the prisoners. Feliz took advantage of the confusion. Popping out one of his claws, he pried apart the chain that held his collar to the others. "Pudding, you need to get out of here quickly while you have time," he barked at the chocolate-brown cat.

"Not on your life," she shouted back. "That degenerate has my cousin in there." She bolted into the old windmill to chase after Meyer and Muse.

~

Lucius Jr. was worried. The unexpected arrival of Frankie and his reinforcements had made the outcome of the day unclear. He began to think of ways to salvage what he could of his victory. That meant Caterwaul had to go.

"Bugsy!" he yelled to his henchman. "I need you to finish him off now. We don't have time to mess around anymore."

Bugsy understood. There would be no more toying. Caterwaul was pretty beaten up, but the big yellow cat had been playing around up until now. He grabbed Caterwaul by the collar then, rising up onto his hind legs, he lifted Caterwaul up with his right front paw until his face was close enough to breathe on.

Caterwaul could clearly see his attacker's droopy eye and mangled ear. He had an amusing yet terrifying thought. As dangerous as this cat was now, how much more effective would he be with two good eyes and ears.

"Boss says it's time to go. I guess that means it's time to go." Bugsy unsheathed the claws on his left forepaw. "It's time for Caterwaul to go to sleep . . . forever."

He drew back his left arm. Caterwaul knew he was done for. One swipe of that powerful left paw, and it was all over. Suddenly he felt the big cat's grip loosen. His one good eye rolled backward, and he yelped in pain. Looking downward, Caterwaul could see his saviors. Juan was slashing furiously at Bugsy's exposed chest while Frankie dug his claws into his legs.

Bugsy staggered and fell forward. As the big yellow cat moved to land on all fours, he let go of his victim. Caterwaul grabbed onto Bugsy's upper arm and with a sudden burst of energy, swung himself onto his back. Grabbing on with his hind legs, Caterwaul slammed his front paws downward into Bugsy's face. His right paw connected with the big cat's nose, while the left tore into the flap of skin covering his remaining good eye.

Virtually blinded and bleeding from his many wounds, Bugsy shook the ragged Caterwaul from his shoulders and staggered off, howling into the woods.

~

Pudding was raging. She'd watched that piece of trash Meyer drag Muse back into the old windmill only minutes before. She had no way of knowing if they were still inside or if Meyer had hauled her out the back and vanished. The lanterns that lit the building had, for the most part, burned themselves out. The only light remaining came from a few last flickering candles and the moon. She heard something coming up behind her, and she spun around with her claws bared.

"Shhh . . . easy now, it's just me. I'm here to help." It was Feliz. He signaled for her to be quiet. Whispering to her, he asked, "Which way did they go?"

"I'm not sure," she answered. "Maybe up, maybe out."

There was noise coming from the room where the cushions were. Carefully Pudding and Feliz moved forward toward the sound, but when they got there, they found it was only Gerhard trying to get to his feet. Just then, they both caught a glimpse of a shadowy figure moving toward the stairway.

"Get Gerhard to safety," said Feliz. "I'll go after whoever that was."

Pudding wrapped the injured Gerhard's paw across her shoulders and led him out through the back door.

~

Outside the old windmill, the fight was drawing to a close. With Bugsy and Meyer out of the fracas, the momentum quickly shifted from the Felinos to Frankie and his men. Lucius Jr. could not believe it. With a sweep of his eyes, he could see most of his crew had been beaten up pretty badly. How was he ever going to explain this to his father? After a disaster like this, there was no way the old man would let him succeed him as *capo di tutti gatte.*

He needed to get out of there. Moving with a stealth one could never imagine from a cat of his build, Jr. slipped from the battlefield to the area behind the windmill. A smile returned to his face when he saw Pudding and Gerhard before him, defenseless. At least it wouldn't be a total loss. He could get rid of Gerhard for good and take the chocolate female as a hostage.

He brought out his claws and readied himself to pounce. But before he could launch himself, something grabbed him and yanked him away. It was something big and wet with a massive set of teeth. It was Huxley, and he had the fat cat engulfed in his jaws. From high up on the hound's back came a voice. "I'd love to see you try to get out of this one Jr." Straddling the big dog's neck, grabbling onto his collar, was Coy the kitten. He was laughing triumphantly. He slid down to the ground as Huxley gripped the terrified Felino tightly in his jaws and shook him.

Gerhard grabbed his hat off Lucius Jr.'s head. "I believe that this belongs to me," he said.

"Better late than never," said Coy with a chuckle. He extended his paw in friendship. "Hi, I'm Coy . . . I'm glad to see the party's still happening."

~

Feliz caught up with the shadowy figure on the windmill's fourth level. It was a medium-sized cat, but that was about all he could be sure of in the darkness. The figure seemed to be dangling from something overhead and apparently had not yet caught Feliz's scent, too busy at the moment to notice his approach. Feliz flung himself at the swinging cat, landing across his chest. He then drew his claws and sneered. "I guess you're not as tough as you thought you were, eh, Meyer?"

"I guess not," said the cat underneath, "But there's only one problem with your logic . . . I'm not Meyer." In the sparse light of the moon coming through the window above them, Feliz could now see the cat beneath him was not a stripy. He was all black. He had just tackled Caterwaul.

"Get off me, Feliz," said Caterwaul. "I need your help." Feliz put his talons away and helped Caterwaul to his feet. "Up there on that nail, there is a pack. It's very important to me. But after the mauling I just took from Bugsy, I don't have the strength left to jump up to that ledge to get it."

Feliz had no trouble with that request. He was relatively undamaged from the night's events. He hopped up onto the ledge and handed Caterwaul his pack. Caterwaul opened it up and withdrew a pouch full of his salve and a small canister of liquid. He drank down a little more than half the liquid and then passed the container to his friend. Feliz looked at him curiously.

"Go ahead," said Caterwaul. "Drink it. It will help restore your strength." He grabbed a handful of the salve and started smearing it onto his wounds. It had a really strong odor, and Feliz wrinkled his nose. The black cat pushed the packet over to Feliz. "If you have any cuts or scrapes or open wounds of any kind, put some of this on it. And when you're done, I need you to put some on my back. I can't reach it."

This surely is a strange cat, thought Feliz, but he did as he was instructed. Almost immediately, he started to feel better, but he wasn't too sure he liked the strong smell of wintergreen that now emanated from his body.

Caterwaul searched through the contents of his pack. He was certain he had brought with him a packet of the Witch's spell reviver. But it was nowhere to be found. *I must have forgotten it,* he thought. That meant if he needed to use any kind of actual magic spell, it would completely wipe him out energy-wise.

"No magic for me today," he mumbled quietly to himself.

The two cats searched the remaining upper levels thoroughly, but there was no sign of Muse or her captor. While they were on the sixth level, they heard a tremendous racket from below, followed by what sounded like a wooden door slamming shut. Whoever it was had been hiding below the trapdoor to the basement.

"Will somebody please help me?" It was the cry of a female cat. Caterwaul and Feliz ran to the edge of the platform just in time to see Meyer dragging the screaming Muse through the back exit.

"Come on!" shouted Caterwaul, as the two cats turned and ran back down the stairs.

By the time they got down and through the door, Meyer and Muse had vanished. But ahead of them in the grass they could hear moaning. Moving toward the source, they could see a white cat lying in the grass.

"Muse!" shouted Caterwaul as he ran to the fallen cat.

"No," said the cat shaking his head. It was Frankie, and he was bleeding from a large bite on his neck. "We have got to stop meeting like this," said Frankie.

"Meyer?" Caterwaul asked him. Frankie nodded.

"They went that way." Frankie pointed in the direction behind him. "Watch out for his teeth. They're really big. I swear I've never seen a set of fangs like that on a cat before."

"We should be able to catch up with them pretty quickly," said Feliz. "He can't move too fast with Muse slowing him down."

"That's what I'm afraid of," Caterwaul replied. "In order to get away, he might just do something awful to her and leave her to die."

After about fifteen minutes they came to a clearing. There,

tied tightly to a tree, was Muse. There were a handful of leaves shoved in her mouth to prevent her from calling out, but her wide blue eyes were filled with terror. Feliz ran forward to cut her down.

"Feliz . . . no!" screamed Caterwaul. "It's a trap."

Before he even finished that sentence, Meyer sprang. He had been lying in ambush on a tree limb. He caught Feliz completely by surprise and started wailing away with his claws. Before Caterwaul could move to help, Meyer drew back his gums revealing his massive teeth. Two strategic bites to Feliz' shoulders were all it took to incapacitate the impetuous feline.

Meyer turned toward Caterwaul. "Looks like it's just you and me now, cupcake," he hissed at Muse's would-be rescuer. "This is gonna be hysterectical." He pointed to his head. "I know you're a smart kitty cat. But I don't imagine you've quite the fighting skills of your now parapalegical friend there.

"You know what I'm gonna do to ya now?" he asked, not expecting an answer. "I'm gonna immortally wound you. That's so as you die real slow like. Then I'm gonna make you watch as I distemper your girlfriend here right in front of your eyes. Then finally," he flashed his fangs at Caterwaul, "I'm gonna tear you into teensy little bits with my saber teeth." Meyer's fur and tail were at attention. He was hissing. The stripy looked positively insane as he stepped toward Caterwaul. Then a shadow passed over the Felino's head and he looked up, just in time to see the huge, toothy open mouth of Huxley looming over him.

"Mine are bigger," said the hound as he brought his head down on the gangster and gobbled him up.

~

The following afternoon, Caterwaul woke up next to Muse on a cushion inside the old windmill. There were cats everywhere, some awake and milling about, some still sleeping.

Muse was already awake, rested and staring at him with her big blue eyes. "I like watching you sleep," she said stroking his fur. "You make the sweetest purring sound when you sleep."

Caterwaul sat up. Much of the night before was still a blur. He wasn't sure what was real and what was a dream. "Meyer? What happened to Meyer?" he asked.

Coy, who was running toward him, answered his question. "Huxley happened to him, that's what." Coy had a big old smile on his face. "Glad to see you're okay, pal," he said.

"But how did you guys find us?"

Coy started to laugh. "That was easy. Whatever that goop is you put on to help heal your wounds, it stinks. I could smell it a mile away. So, for a dog with a sniffer like Huxley's, it was a piece of cake."

Caterwaul got to his feet and walked outside; Muse and Coy followed him. Out on the grass in front of the old windmill, Frankie was singing a song. He had three other cats singing harmonies and an audience of six or seven cats listening intently.

Frankie wasn't just boasting, Caterwaul thought. *He is really very good.* He gave the crooner a wave of his paw in thanks, and Frankie nodded.

"I'm going have to get that cat to come sing at the castle someday," Caterwaul said.

"The castle?" asked Muse. "That's the second time you mentioned that horrible place. What do you have to do with the castle?"

Caterwaul answered her. "What if I told you that Cathoon is no longer the dreary, desolate place you think it is, and that the queen has changed? She has been a good friend to me.

She's even allowed me to transform the castle into a beautiful sanctuary for cats," he said. "It's my home. Come with me, and I'll show you."

Muse scoffed. "Bugsy must've hit you even harder than I thought, and you are out of your cat head. Queen Druciah, a cat lover? You sure have an active imagination, my love. It was Queen Druciah who sent that man to take my mother away from me all those years ago."

"Trust me, it's all true. She is different now."

"If it were only true, then I would love to take you up on your previous offer. I have never had a five-course dinner, especially not one prepared by a gourmet chef." Muse pondered the possibility that the queen had changed. She shook her head because she did not believe it.

"Come to the castle then in five days, and I'll show you," Caterwaul boasted. "I will have Orris make you the most amazing meal you have ever tasted. You will see that what I say is true. Muse, the queen is going to love you as much as she loves me."

At that point, Muse could not doubt him. He had saved her life. She was in love with her furry black hero and would follow him to the end of the earth if he asked her to.

"Very well, my Caterwaul," she said. "I will see you at the castle in five days." She leaned forward and kissed him on his nose.

Caterwaul was ecstatic, but he was also in tremendous pain. He was so badly beaten up that he could hardly walk. Even if he had not gone ten rounds with the strongest cat on the planet, he would need at least two days to get back to Cathoon. So he said goodbye to Pudding and Gerhard, and the brothers too.

To Frankie, he promised a chance to sing at the castle one day in the not too distant future. The two cats embraced and swore to remain friends forever. He made sure there were no Felinos lying around loose and left the job of taking care of Lucius Jr. in the capable paws of Coy and his new friend Huxley.

Then after a final farewell to Muse, he started to walk away. As soon as he was completely out of sight, he said, "That's enough of this." He uttered a few words of incantation and disappeared.

22

Back at the Castle

Caterwaul felt the cold water rush over him, and he shot to attention.

"Get up!" a voice shouted at him. It was the queen, and she was fuming. "You've been lying there for more than two days, cat. I've been screaming at you, shaking you, and this is the third time my guards have thrown water on you. Yet you just lie there. You were gone more than a week. What news do you have for me? Were you able to locate the all-white female cat as I instructed?"

Druciah paced frantically around the room, and she rubbed her face. "I found three more awful hairs this morning," she shouted, "and what on earth has happened to that oaf Warwick Vane Bezel III? He's been gone for days now, too, with no word. That's not like him at all. I have work for him. I need him." She was gravely distressed.

Caterwaul could only interpret her hostility as a reaction to his "sleeping off period." Performing any powerful spell, such as the one which teleported him from near the old windmill to here, required a certain amount of recovery time. Still, for him to have slept for nearly two days had to be because of his injuries.

"Well . . . tell me. Did you find her?" Druciah demanded.

"As a matter of fact I did," he said. "Her name is Muse, and she is the most incredible cat I have ever seen in my life. She is smart and beautiful and just perfect in every way." Caterwaul tingled when he talked about her. "She will be arriving in . . . let's see, you said I was asleep for two days . . ." he quickly did the math, "in three days time."

All of a sudden Druciah's outward personality changed completely. A huge smile came across her face as she lifted Caterwaul up and grabbed him in a big hug. She was squeezing a little too tightly, and Caterwaul attempted to squirm free.

"My wonderful amazing cat," she gushed. "I knew I could count on you. Three days . . . I don't know how I will last that long without meeting her."

Caterwaul was no fool. He had a suspicion that something was up from the way her emotions flipped so easily from foul to fair.

"I've invited her to dinner at the castle," he said. "I told her that Orris is the finest chef in all the land."

"Well, of course he is, my dear," she said with a smirk. "He works for me doesn't he? You don't think I would employ anyone but the best to cook for me, do you?" She was elated. Finally she was going to have her youth back.

"You go ahead and rest, my friend. You have made your queen very happy, and you have a big day coming up. In the meantime, I will meet with Orris to discuss the menu for our upcoming feast. We will pull out all the stops and spare no expense. After all, we must make sure it's a night your lovely Muse will never forget."

As she slipped away, Caterwaul shook his head. Something was just not right at Castle Cathoon. The queen was acting strangely. In fact, ever since she returned from the Red Moon Forest, she had not been the same. He loved her very much and wanted to trust her, but the queen was not the same woman he had befriended and with whom he shared a home.

Caterwaul decided he should keep a close eye on his "beloved queen."

~

Pudding ran up to Muse excitedly. There were only two more days until her cousin would be reunited with her heroic Caterwaul. Neither of the females had ever been invited to a royal function before, and they really had no inkling how to prepare. Muse wanted to make the best impression possible so that the queen would like her.

Because Pudding had been a dressmaker, she knew something of fashion. In the home in which they lived, there were all manner of bangles, bows, and strips of colored ribbon. The chocolate-colored kitty wanted to make sure her cousin was the fairest cat in all the land when she showed up at the castle for the feast.

You see, Pudding knew her cousin was in love. She had never seen Muse so happy. It was more than just the fact that he had saved her life, although that would usually be enough to encourage devotion. There was something special about Caterwaul. He was one in a million, the kind of cat who really stood for something, and both she and her cousin knew it.

Since they both had once been human, they both retained the human fascination for dressing up. They spent hours trying on different variations of ribbons and collars and costume jewels. After all, they had been teenagers just a few short weeks before.

"I think that's just perfect," said Pudding, admiring her handiwork. Muse looked absolutely amazing. She was wearing a beautiful ribbon of cerulean blue, which looped in a bow at her breast. Her collar was covered in jewels they had scavenged from one of the homes of another transformee. Her hair was styled perfectly, and her face beamed with the joy of new love.

"Do you think the queen will like me, cousin?" asked Muse.

"How could she not?" replied Pudding reassuringly. "You are the most beautiful cat I have ever seen, and you are twice as lovely inside as out. If she doesn't adore you as Caterwaul does, it will be because she has no heart. But your Caterwaul would never stay with someone with no heart, so it follows she will love you."

The smile on Muse's face was electric. She hopped up on a chair to see herself in the mirror. It was the same mirror that had changed her weeks ago. *That was the best day of my life,* she thought. She would never go back, even if she could.

~

Druciah was humming to herself as she moved along the corridors of her huge and empty castle. She was overjoyed and full of herself. The queen was so happy she was practically dancing as she glided down the passageway toward the kitchen, where she knew Orris, her chef, was waiting.

"Orris, my dear, the day is nigh upon us," she shouted down the hall. "We will at long last be having company. The day after tomorrow my loyal servant Caterwaul is introducing us to the most perfect specimen of a pure-white female cat in all the land."

Under her breath she added, "And I will have my beauty once again."

She was puffed up with confidence that her plan was bearing fruit as she strode into the kitchen, where her chef was hard at work preparing for the feast to come.

"Is everything ready?" she asked.

"Yes, your majesty. I have done everything you asked."

His head was down. He had been around Druciah enough in Caterwaul's absence to know she was planning something, and he was not at all happy about being a part of what he felt soon would be the betrayal of a friend.

Over the time they spent together, Orris had grown to respect and care about the black feline. Caterwaul had brought a sense of fun back into this tedious castle existence. He wasn't sure exactly what was in the queen's mind, but he knew her well enough to be suspicious.

"Good," she said, "show me what you've done."

"Your majesty, I have prepared the sauce to your specifications, and now I am working on the crust. I must admit I was worried about some of the ingredients. As you might have imagined, I've never worked with salamanders or the toes of rats before, so you will excuse me if I had my doubts. But I assure you the end result . . . *c'est magnifique.*" He brought his thumb and index finger together in a loop and kissed them as he said these final words.

"As far as the crust goes, I have dispatched one of your best men to procure the honey necessary to sweeten the dough, because I know that you are not fond of caramel."

"Excellent," she said expectantly. "Then things are almost ready. All we need now is the main ingredient, and it will be delivered soon."

"But what is the main ingredient, your majesty?" he asked her respectfully. "After all these years I have worked for you, is it too much to ask to know the main ingredient featured in this pie?"

"Why, Orris, it is the tail of a pure-white female cat," she answered him excitedly. "And she will be arriving very soon." She giggled insanely with her own cleverness, while across from her, Orris bowed his head in shame.

From his position safely hidden on the shelf behind the spice jars, Caterwaul witnessed this entire exchange. He thought he was going to be sick. Everything he thought and felt about this queen was a lie. She was clearly out of her mind.

Her aging and vain obsession had completely put her psyche out of balance.

While he thought he was bringing a guest to his home to enjoy the hospitality of the castle, he was actually leading his darling Muse into a trap. Druciah had used him the entire time. And now it was clear that Orris was also involved. This puzzled him and caused him to choke. He wondered how Orris could be any part of such a plan. While he sat there in hiding, sickened, the queen turned giddily toward the entrance to the room and left.

Well, Caterwaul had news for the queen. Things were not going to go the way she'd planned. Not if he had anything to say about it.

23

Feline Pie

Caterwaul would not let the queen out of his sight. He knew she had terrible plans for his beloved Muse. Those plans included the taking of her tail. There was no way he was going to let that happen—he would stop her.

He was a cat and, therefore, naturally surefooted, but his experiences of the last week or so had made him craftier and more catlike than he'd been in years. He really felt alive, and all this clandestine activity really got his blood flowing.

He was spying on her the day that Muse was set to arrive. He overheard Druciah telling her chef what he was to do once the white cat got there. From what Caterwaul could gather, Druciah had acquired some kind of drug, which she wanted Orris to put into the dessert course of the five-course meal. With both Caterwaul and Muse unconscious from this drug, Druciah intended for Orris to then come in and take Muse's tail.

Caterwaul shook violently at the thought of his Muse losing her tail.

Then he smiled because he realized that all he had to do was make sure the sedative never made it into their food.

Still, he couldn't understand why Orris, of all people, would turn on him. Orris had been his friend, and he thought, perhaps foolishly, that he had been the one to bring substance back into the cook's life. The cat decided to hide in the kitchen for a while to watch him.

What Caterwaul saw was a man torn. He was stretched thinly between his loyalty to his queen, which was owed by right and custom, and the loyalty to his friend, which was owed by what was in his heart. Flustered, the chef held the bottle of the elixir in his hand. He turned it over and over repeatedly trying to decide which course was the best to take.

Finally he made up his mind. He could not do it. He slammed the crystal bottle on the counter and went off in search of his friend.

Caterwaul waited until Orris had left the kitchen before jumping down. The bottle was small, and its stopper was fitted with an eyedropper. Caterwaul was able to grasp the bottle and hook the stopper through his collar. Setting the vial squarely between his shoulders, he was able to carry it off.

~

On his way to follow Orris, Caterwaul encountered the queen. "Are you excited to see your lovely friend Muse, my love?" she asked.

"Yes, of course I am, my queen," he said. "I miss her. It's been far too many days since the last time I saw her."

"Well," said Druciah, "she will be here tomorrow afternoon and I promise you that she will be treated like a princess. I do so enjoy the company of cats, much more than that of other humans."

"Thank you, your majesty. You have been very good to me," said Caterwaul excusing himself.

"Oh and Caterwaul," added the queen, "make sure to remove the spell from all of the mirrors, won't you, my darling?"

"Of course, your majesty," he said.

~

Caterwaul found the chef sitting on the narrow bridge over the koi pond. He was looking sad and forlorn. "You look like a man with a lot on his mind," Caterwaul opened.

Orris just looked at him with that sadness in his eyes.

"Caterwaul, you and I are friends."

"I have come to believe so," the cat answered.

"Well . . . I have something I must tell you."

"I know."

Orris was puzzled. "You . . . you know?"

"You, my friend, face a dilemma. You have been told to do something by the queen, your mistress, which you know with all of your heart and soul to be wrong. Am I right on this, Orris?" Orris shook his head in answer, yes.

"But I know what the queen will do to me if I do not follow her orders. Servants quickly find themselves to be ex-servants, or worse." Orris thought of the castle's former chef Elias and the hair. It made him giggle for only a second, and then he was dead serious again.

"Let me get this straight. You were ordered to cut off the tail of the white cat, correct?"

Again the chef nodded.

Well then, it seems that we need to make sure you have a white cat to work with." Caterwaul smiled. "You just leave that to me."

~

Pudding arranged for Muse to travel with a procession on her journey to Cathoon Castle. The furry brown cat had two reasons for this. First, there was still the possibility that the Felinos were out there ready to cause mischief, and second, she believed that anyone traveling to visit the queen should travel with an escort. It was just the classy thing to do.

When Muse left the village for the castle, she did it in style. In her entourage, she brought a friend of Pudding's to dress her, as well as the brothers Juan and Feliz to serve as her protection. It was understood by all that the brothers would only escort her as far as the castle gate, but they felt that this was the least they could do considering what Caterwaul had done to help them in the battle against the Felinos.

Besides, both Juan and Feliz were completely smitten with Pudding, and they would do just about anything to keep her cousin safe, especially if it meant showing off their bravery.

The trip to Cathoon proved uneventful. There were no ambushes or attacks of any kind. Feliz was disappointed. Like most fighters, he liked to keep his skills finely honed. He was expecting, or hoping, to be jumped at least once along the way. Nevertheless, Muse was ecstatic the journey went off without a hitch.

Up ahead, they could see the walls of the castle. Though it was still a good distance away, Muse knew it wouldn't be long before she would see her cherished Caterwaul. She smiled and called to increase the party's pace.

~

In the great room sat the queen. She was dressed in her royal finest. Caterwaul had never seen her dressed so formally before. She really looked regal as she approached him on the day of the feast. Her dress was made of the choicest golden silk from the east, and on her head she wore a crown adorned with the most beautiful and ornately carved gems imaginable. This was to be a day for the ages.

"It won't be long now," she said to her cat companion. "Your Muse will be arriving soon. I certainly hope we have done all we can to fulfill her expectations."

The queen seemed genuine in her good will, but by now Caterwaul knew better. He now knew she had the ability to slip in and out of character at will. It was the way she used people—and cats too, it seemed. There was nothing at all sincere in her appearance. Caterwaul found it just a bit too creepy. He wondered if there ever had been any love in her at all, whether their entire time together had been a sham.

The black cat shook his head. He wanted to believe he had meant something to the queen, but in the long run it didn't matter. Her plan to drug them was exposed. He continued to play along with Druciah for as long as he could stand it.

"You have removed the spell from the mirrors?" she inquired.

"Of course, my queen," he replied. "I am your dedicated servant."

~

It was about teatime when Muse arrived at the castle. Caterwaul met her at the drawbridge. She was even more beautiful than he remembered. He thanked Juan and Feliz for their help in escorting his lady friend all the way from Harsizzle and offered them a room filled with food and water in which to rest. They eagerly accepted this hospitality; neither of them had been to a castle before.

Muse was very glad to see Caterwaul. He looked strong and rested. All of the wear and tear he'd absorbed back at the old windmill was gone. *He really is a handsome cat*, she thought.

"You must give me the grand tour of your home, my love," she begged, grabbing him tightly by the paw. He was delighted to again be with her. As she dragged him forward, she was giggling. Dinner was more than an hour off, so Caterwaul figured he had the time to show her at least some of the sights.

He took her to all of the places he'd redesigned. He brought her to the solarium where they stretched out on the many plush pillows strewn all about. Then they went to the maze of hedges he had planted in the yard and watched the birds as they ate and drank at the special feeders he had designed.

Muse could not believe her eyes. Every room they ventured into came alive with swirls of color and wonderful textured fabrics. Every one of them was filled with various cat playthings. She could see that he'd been right when describing it to her back at the old windmill. This place was a cat paradise.

He showed her rooms designed as testing grounds for cats to improve their strength and conditioning. There were balance beams and vaulting horses. Finally he brought her to his favorite spot, the bridge above the koi pond.

As they sat together on the bridge, their legs dangling over the ledge, he told her his wonderful plans for the future. She beamed at him because, as she'd hoped, those plans included her. She sweetly slid her arm over his shoulders, kissed his cheek, and purred contentedly.

"Never in my wildest dreams could I have imagined this place," she whispered to herself. Cathoon was all he had promised her and more. She was the luckiest kitty in the entire world.

The sun was starting to go down. Caterwaul flicked a dangling paw at one of the huge goldfish below and said, "I believe that it just may be dinnertime."

~

The table in the royal dining hall was beautiful. It was long and opulent, made of brilliantly carved polished hardwood. On top of it were placed three sets of plates and the appropriate silverware for a five-course royal feast. Caterwaul sat at one end of the table and the queen at the other. Muse sat next to Caterwaul on his right. She was shaking with excitement. She could hardly believe she was here.

"How was your journey, young Muse?" asked the queen. "Not too difficult, I hope."

"Oh no, your majesty," Muse answered. "It wasn't difficult at all. The weather was wonderful and the scenery magnificent. We had no trouble making excellent time along the way. But then I had some excellent escorts who knew how much I wanted to see Caterwaul again."

Muse looked down the table to where the queen sat holding a glass of wine.

"And you also . . . your majesty. I want to thank you from the bottom of my heart for the generous invitation." The queen acknowledged her respectfully with a smile and a nod.

Then Muse continued, "Your home is the most wonderful place I could ever imagine; yet for years, everyone has spoken of this place with horror."

The queen, unused to criticism of any kind, became agitated.

"Yet as Caterwaul told me, and more importantly, has shown me, the fears and concerns of Harsizzle are obviously unfounded. Every part of your castle that my love has shown me is incredible. I say to you, my queen, that you have been portrayed unfairly. I consider it my duty to tell the world they have been wrong about you."

Druciah grinned with the impression of gratitude. "Thank you, Muse. My association with Caterwaul has helped me to grow more than I ever could have imagined. It is because of him that I have allowed my home to be opened to things I never could have imagined." She hid her disgust regarding Caterwaul's "improvements" masterfully.

"You, my queen, are a true friend of cats everywhere." Muse curtseyed to Druciah with honest respect.

~

Orris brought them the first course at a quarter after six. It was a delicate creamy soup made with mushrooms, root vegetables, and some type of shellfish. The smell coming from the terrine was heavenly. Both Caterwaul and his companion were in awe. Orris was a truly gifted man in the kitchen.

Muse dipped her spoon into the bowl and withdrew a huge piece of what must have been crabmeat and popped it into her mouth. For a few seconds, she felt slightly ashamed. This was truly a soup for royalty. *Nobody eats like this in Harsizzle,* thought Muse, as she licked her lips and cleaned her bowl of every drop.

Then she thought, *there is no need for me to feel guilty.* After all, she had been invited, and so, she would make sure she enjoyed every morsel of this fantastic meal. Next came the salad course and, about ten minutes after that, the "officially designated" appetizer.

Caterwaul did not usually care for salad. But this one was topped with tiny, delicate anchovies. Caterwaul gorged himself on the little fishes, while leaving the greens and other vegetables untouched. Muse, a much more civil and lady-like diner, savored the offering in the manner in which it was intended.

The appetizer was a stuffed and roasted pigeon breast. Though for Druciah, this was of appropriate size, for the cats it proved to be enormous. Caterwaul and his date each tasted a few mouthfuls, but then they retired it. After all, there were still two more plates to come.

As the entrée was delivered, Caterwaul noticed that in the back of the dining hall, a doorway opened and two of the queen's guards entered, pushing between them a large mirror covered by a silk spread. It was the mirror from her private chambers.

Muse was too enraptured by the delicious meal to notice anything that was not on a plate. She was in the palace of food heaven and determined to enjoy every bite. She kept looking down the table toward the queen, who would continue to smile and encourage her.

For their main course, Orris had prepared one of his specialties, a pan seared filet of trout with a crawfish cream sauce. It was the queen's favorite dish. Caterwaul knew that the queen had pulled out all the stops to make this meal one for the ages, but he wondered why? Perhaps deep inside she felt some guilt about what she was doing. *Perhaps*, he thought, but he couldn't trust her at all anymore.

Once they had all eaten as much of the fish as they could handle, the queen stood up and asked, "My dearest Muse, have you enjoyed your visit to our castle today?"

Muse was completely stuffed full of food. "Oh yes, your highness," she said, and bowing her head she added, "Your chef is the most wonderful cook in the entire world. Every single dish he brought out for us was better than the one before."

The queen thanked her for the compliments.

"I dare to say I am so satisfied now that I'm quite sure I could not eat another bite."

"Oh, but you must," said the queen. "No feast is complete until the dessert has been served."

Muse rubbed her belly, which was so full now it was making noises. "Your majesty, I appreciate everything you have done for me. I am stuffed to the point of bursting. I apologize, but don't think I will be able to eat your wonderful dessert."

Caterwaul stared at the queen with hatred in his eyes. She was beginning to squirm a little. Her entire plan rested on the two cats eating the dessert.

"But my fair Muse, you insult me. You must promise me that you will at least try Orris's dessert. He has prepared a mousse of no fewer than four distinct flavors. The least you can do is take a bite or two after this wonderful meal I have served you."

Suddenly, Muse was confused. Up until this moment, she had been having the time of her life. The entire evening had been wonderful. The meal was out of this world. The company was even better. Now, all of a sudden, she felt extremely uncomfortable. The queen's demeanor had changed suddenly and not at all for the better.

Caterwaul squeezed her paw and looked her deep in the eyes to reassure her that he was with her and would not let anything happen. Still, Muse was frightened by this change of events.

"Perhaps we can find the room for a small mouthful?" he said still clutching Muse tightly by the paw.

"Excellent!" shouted the queen. "I will have Orris bring it out at once."

Druciah called to her chef to bring out the dessert course, but he was nowhere to be found. She stood up and walked to the center of the table where a silver bell was positioned. It was the bell she used to summon servants who were not where they were supposed to be.

Muse and Caterwaul could both see this disturbed the queen. After about a minute of her ringing the bell, Orris finally came running out with a serving tray supporting three of the most luxurious desserts imaginable.

Caterwaul leaned close to Muse and whispered in her ear, "Follow my lead."

The queen seemed to return to her normal rhythm as the desserts were placed before her guests on the table. "Just a bite or two," she said. "I mean Orris did go through the trouble of preparing it."

Both cats smiled at the queen at the other end of the table and took a large mouthful, followed by a second.

"You were right your majesty," offered Caterwaul. "It is the best dessert I have ever eaten."

Caterwaul rose from the table, and taking his lady by the hand, he started to walk away. "If you will please excuse us, my queen? I'm having trouble keeping my eyes open." He and Muse staggered halfway down the length of the dining hall and suddenly fell over in a pile.

Druciah waited a minute to make sure they were knocked out, and then she started giggling with delight. She had done it. She had pulled it off. For a minute or two, it appeared to be touch-and-go, but then Caterwaul came through for her.

Good old Caterwaul. He had always been a loyal friend to her. It was too bad she had agreed to return him to the Witch. He had been exceptionally useful, even if he did turn her home into a circus attraction.

Oh well, she thought. *It will soon all be over. I will have my youth and beauty back, and Caterwaul will be back with the Witch in that horrible cave.* She swiftly moved to where her guards had placed her mirror. One last look at this ancient bag of bones, she thought. In no time at all, she would be young and beautiful again, and this time, it would be for nine lifetimes.

She pulled the silken covering from the mirror and stared into it. As she did this, she instantaneously transformed into a cat, but not just any cat. She was white from the top of her head to the tip of her tail. The queen was one hundred percent, pure white.

"No!" she screamed. "Curse you, Caterwaul. You told me you had released the spell!"

"I lied." It was Caterwaul's voice from behind her. Spinning around, the queen quickly surmised that neither Caterwaul nor Muse was even close to unconsciousness, Caterwaul hurled himself at Druciah and grabbed her by the face and collar.

Hauling her up onto her haunches, he pulled out the eyedropper he had concealed earlier.

"I believe this is what you thought had been put into our desserts." He squeezed the bulb with all his might, and at least ten drops of the Witch's elixir spurted into her mouth and down her throat.

"No . . . Caterwaul. I love . . . you . . . Why?" her voice trailed off as she fell to the floor, asleep.

"You love me?" he asked mockingly. "That's a laugh. The only one that you love . . . that you are even capable of showing real love to, your highness, is yourself."

"Come on," he called to Muse. "We have to go now." The chef was coming back. Caterwaul waved to Muse to follow, and they dashed out of the dining hall.

Moments later, Orris returned carrying a silver chafing dish. Entering the room, he saw before him the queen, now transformed, lying on the floor in a sound sleep. Scooping up the unconscious white cat with his arms, he carried her back to the kitchen where he had only moments before he placed a sharp cleaver.

"Don't worry my lovely," he said, "this won't hurt a bit." He pulled back his right arm and brought it forward so that the sharp edge of the meat cleaver came down exactly as he wanted it to. He hacked the tail from the sleeping white cat in one expeditious swing. Then he bound the wound.

Epilogue

Orris was almost finished cleaning up the kitchen when he heard a strange sound out in the hallway. He touched the golden top of his pie to see if it had cooled sufficiently before setting it aside. It was getting late, and the hall was almost completely black. The chef lit a torch to see what was going on. As he crept down the hallway to investigate, a cold rush of wind surged past him, extinguishing his torch.

The castle was a fairly spooky place on any night, but tonight it was especially so. There had been no sign of either the queen or Caterwaul for hours. And now this wind he felt in the darkness made it very uncomfortable for him to even be there.

Turning back to the kitchen to relight his torch, he saw the shape of an old woman, dressed completely in black, coalesce from vapors before his eyes. Spotting the limp body of the now tailless queen/cat lying on the dish on the counter, the spirit lifted her up and put the sleeping animal in a large leather carrying case. As she turned to make her exit, Orris attempted to stop her.

"Who are you old woman, and what are you doing with that cat?" He was holding a large spoon and shaking like a leaf as he asked this. He was scared out of his wits. Her lack of make-up frightful hairstyle, and unattractive shoes could mean one thing only. This intruder was none other than the Witch of Red Moon Forest he'd heard so much about. Although, to Orris, she didn't appear to be particularly overweight.

She stared coldly and silently into his eyes. Then as if reading his mind, she squawked, "I've been dieting. I'm trying to drop a few."

Lifting up his cooling pie plate, he asked the Witch, "Would you like a slice of fe . . . fe . . . feline pie? It's only freshly b . . . b . . . baked this evening m . . . madam?"

The Witch glanced at the cook with bored disgust. "Never touch the stuff," she grunted. After muttering some long forgotten words and gesturing in the air, she smiled at the cook with her mouthful of yellow and missing teeth. Then she vanished in a flash of smoke, taking the queen with her.

~

Caterwaul was stretched out on one of the balance beams in the exercise room. He was unusually high up, but for some reason, he wanted to be alone for a bit. From this position, he could look down and see perhaps a hundred or more cats milling about, flirting with one another, having deep conversations, or just playing with the countless squeaky toys and ropes that seemed to be everywhere. These were his subjects now. *It will take me awhile to get used to that*, he thought.

Everything around him was good. His tail swayed back and forth like a more prehensile version of a dog's.

"Caterwaul, watch this," came a voice from behind him. Pushing himself up onto his claws, he reversed his position on the beam. It was Muse, and she was swinging from a set of rings. He watched her awhile as she swung back and forth. On each move forward, she arched her back and pushed her hind legs out in front of her to gain momentum. Then, once she reached what she believed was her maximum safe altitude, she let go of the rings and did a twisting back flip before landing softly on the mats below.

Caterwaul clapped his paws. She made a perfect four-point landing. "That was fantastic, Muse," he said, all the while continuing the applause. "You're really becoming quite the gymnast." He hopped down from his place on the balance beam to walk with her.

"It's very important that we all try to stay in the very best shape possible," he said, as he rubbed her back. He was especially happy to see her conquering her former fears. Every time she pushed her personal envelope, she gained the confidence to do more. It was good for her to be around so many cats that were unafraid to take risks. In fact, he knew she enjoyed the rush she felt from these new experiences. Caterwaul wanted her to be prepared for the next time trouble came along.

He was serious. Though for now it seemed that life was good in the castle, Caterwaul knew it was only a matter of time before something happened to threaten their idyllic lives.

The Felinos were still in control of much of Harsizzle, including the village docks and fish stocks. The fact that Coy and Huxley took out Meyer bought them some breathing room, but he wasn't fool enough to consider it a lasting solution.

And what about still unknown threats they may not be prepared for? Surely by now the word had spread to other villages that the Felinos can be beaten. It was only a matter of time before someone decided to test the waters. Caterwaul was frightened about these outsiders who might come to Harsizzle to make their fortunes.

Nor did he assume that they'd seen the last of Druciah. He knew the queen was not completely defeated; she was merely transformed. Somewhere, Caterwaul knew she was hiding out, biding her time, and plotting her revenge on the ones who thwarted her scheme to achieve immortality. The hunter was still a question- mark too. Surely he could not be happy that Huxley had run off without his permission.

Though all these thoughts concerned him, the biggest question running through his brain was the whereabouts of police commander Warwick Vane Bezel III. What had happened to him since the episode with the cart? The last time any cat had seen the commander was when Gerhard had found him locked in the cage, naked. When Coy and Huxley had returned to the cage to investigate, Warwick was gone. Caterwaul was concerned. Did the Felino's have him—or possibly, somebody worse?

Oh well, he thought, these were far too many depressing things to occupy the mind of a cat. Especially on this day, which was supposed to be a celebration. He put on his "worry-free" face and attempted to enjoy himself. Today was the day he would officially be recognized as the lord of the lands and ruler of the castle. Every cat who was any cat was expected to come to his coronation party that evening.

His friends Juan and Feliz were hired to run the security for the event. Though he trusted them implicitly, Caterwaul swore that he had seen among the security recruits several former members of the Felino Gang. There weren't any "made" felines among them, just low-level muscle, but still it worried him, bringing his former enemies into the fold so soon.

Taking Juan aside, Caterwaul questioned the logic of having former Felino associates on the payroll. Juan laughed and said he'd checked each of them out thoroughly and none of these cats had really done much harm. Every one of them pledged loyalty to Caterwaul and swore to protect the realm. Juan told him he felt these few "fellas" deserved the chance to redeem themselves.

Frankie and his band were scheduled to perform a few sets of the classics, and were rehearsing in the great hall. Caterwaul and Muse strolled down the castle halls to watch them as they ran through their song list for the evening. Caterwaul went straight up to the crooner and threw his arms around him.

"What do you think?" Caterwaul asked his friend.

"This whole place is the cat's pajamas," said Frankie. "To tell you the truth, I can't believe I'm here. Thanks, Cat . . . " he paused in mid-sentence. He wasn't sure how he should properly address his friend, now that he was going to be a lord.

"Help me out a bit here, pal . . . what's a simple cat like me supposed to call you, now that you've become a lord and all?"

Caterwaul laughed and hugged the crooner tightly. "My friend, you can always call me Caterwaul; we've no titles or formalities between us. You and I bled together in battle, Frankie. That gives us a special bond that can never be broken."

Frankie smiled. "But tell me, what are we going to do about tonight? As I understand it, you want us to set up here in the great hall to play for the maximum number of citizens possible."

Caterwaul nodded.

"But your majest . . . eh, sorry . . . Caterwaul . . . the room isn't near ready. I mean the stage hasn't even been built yet."

"Don't you worry about that, friend. Everything is under control. I have a guy coming to specifically take charge of organizing the entire room for tonight, and believe me, he comes under the highest recommendation."

At that moment, the enormous doors of the great hall swung open and in strode an enormous man-sized snapping turtle and two beavers. The snapping turtle was wrapped in a thin silk jacket with gold and purple streamers covering his shell. He wore clear lip-gloss on his beak, long false eyelashes, oh yes . . . and a colorful scarf about his neck.

"Never fear, Joffrey is here!" shouted the turtle as way of announcing himself. As he spoke, he threw his arms widely into the air. "You have a problem? My assssssociates and I can handle anything. You fellas have a job for me?" He approached the area where Frankie and Caterwaul stood.

Looking down at Frankie, Joffrey spoke. "Do I have the pleasure of addressing the new lord and master of all the land?" he asked.

Frankie started to laugh. "Not me, sweetheart," he pointed to Caterwaul. "He's the one you wanna see."

"Pardon me, your highness . . . I just asssssumed . . ." he stopped himself short, realizing what he said might be perceived as an insult. Then he suddenly recognized Caterwaul from his days with the Witch in the forest. Smiling, the turtle said, "Moving up in the world, I sssee. Tell me, your lordship, what do you need for us to do?"

Caterwaul quickly explained to the turtle that the room was going to be used for his affirmation party, and it needed to be done up quickly.

Joffrey spun around and snapped his enormous claws together. The sound echoed off the castle's stone walls, and suddenly everyone quieted down.

Looking at his companions he said, "Okay . . . Woody I need you to grab as many of these cats as you need and ssstart working on the ssstage area. You, Castor, will be responsible for getting the musicians together and making ssssure their equipment is all ssset up, in tune, and ready for them to play. Am I clear, guys?" The two beavers nodded and silently set to work.

Caterwaul was stunned that Joffrey was able to quiet things down with just a click of his nails.

"Well, I am a sssnapping turtle," he giggled, then said humorously, "oh sssnap."

The reptilian designer continued. "Now I will handle the room decoration while Carlos takes care of the sssnack situation."

"Carlos?" asked Caterwaul. "Who's Carlos? There were only the three of you when you came in together."

"No sssilly, there were four." He started to count on his claws and realized the cat was right. This set him off. Where in the world was Carlos?

"Carlos!" he shouted. "We've lost Carlos again!" He turned back to Caterwaul. "I ssswear I can't let him out of my sssight for even a sssecond . . . You don't by any chance have a creek around here anywhere?"

~

That night, the affirmation party was a huge success. Everyone Caterwaul could have wanted there was present. The great hall was packed with animals of all shapes and sizes. There were even some humans from the village who came to recognize that a new era was dawning in the land.

Coy was stretched out on Huxley's enormous back with two cute young females. He knew how to milk this hero thing pretty well. They oohed and aahed as he showed them his scars and told them the story of how he singlehandedly rescued more than fifty cats from certain death at the hand of the hunter. It didn't hurt that the dog they were lying on was there as "a witness" to corroborate his every exaggeration. Huxley played his part expertly.

Even Gerhard was there. He'd recovered enough from his many injuries to make the journey. When he presented himself before the new lord, he introduced Caterwaul to his new girlfriend. She was exactly what Caterwaul expected, a big, strong, meaty, long-haired calico. Gerhard introduced her as Sunny.

Later on, as the party progressed, Caterwaul could not help himself. He had to take a look. After dropping something "accidentally on purpose," his eyes moved along the ground to see if she did indeed meet Gerhard's prerequisite.

Caterwaul looked at his friend and smiled. He made a sign with his paws that Sunny did indeed have very small ankles.

"Uh huh," Gerhard affirmed. "That's good breedin'."

~

Orris was in a full-on cooking frenzy. It had been years since he had been forced to work this hard. He was constantly blowing the hair from the front of his face and wiping perspiration from his forehead. He'd hired six assistants just to help him with the day's events and that didn't include the four-legged ones.

That didn't mean he wasn't happy, though. In fact, he was ecstatic, glad to be back in his element. This was what he'd always loved about working in the castle, the hustle and bustle of a feast in full swing. He was back in his domain, and he had Caterwaul to thank for it.

~

Out in the great hall, the music flowed like the food coming from the kitchen. Joffrey and his two beaver friends pulled off a near miracle. Everything was going perfectly. The stage the beavers built was magnificent and the band had plenty of opportunity to rehearse before the guests started arriving. Of course, the whole general layout of the hall was especially well done, and for that, Caterwaul wanted to personally congratulate the turtle.

The new lord finally found him standing in a corner to the right of the stage. Joffrey had finally given up his search for Carlos and was now deep in a discussion concerning the comparative merits of turtle claws versus cat claws when carving fine furniture. His foil in the discussion? Who else but young Feliz, he of the massively magnificent hand skewers?

"You should come to visit me in the forest sssome time," the turtle said, "Almost everything in my home is hand carved . . . by me, of course. If you have a chance to sssee what I've done, I think you'll be impressed; the detail is amazing."

When they saw Caterwaul coming toward them, they stiffened to a sort of lazy attention. It was obvious that both cat and turtle had overindulged in the castle's hospitality.

"Joffrey," Caterwaul called toward them. "Just the turtle I've been looking for."

The man-sized snapper wasn't sure what was going on. Had he done something wrong? He was certain he had followed protocol. But had he mistakenly done something inappropriate? He wasn't one hundred percent sure, it was true, but he was fairly confident he hadn't accidentally disemboweled any of tonight's party guests.

Joffrey moved toward him with his head down, hoping he hadn't given any offense.

"Joffrey, I just wanted to say that you and your crew have done a fantastic job organizing things for tonight's event. I could really use a reptile of your abilities here at the castle and was wondering if you might like to work for me full-time?"

~

Coy and Huxley were on a mission. They were looking for a ladder. Only hours ago, the place was crawling with workers, and Coy himself counted at least ten ladders in various parts of the castle. But now, there wasn't a single one anywhere to be found.

The little cat was frustrated. "With all of this new construction, you'd think there would be plenty of ladders around."

Coy rode on the big dog's back. The two of them had developed a system where the small kitten could remain aboard even if the hound was moving fast. Right now, the hound was flying through the castle halls. Finally, in one of the sections of the castle furthest from the coronation feast, they spotted a workman. Over his shoulder, he carried the ladder they were looking for.

"Start making as much noise as you can," the kitten yelled to his fast-moving friend. Huxley added barking and drooling to the racket he was already making as he ran. When the workman turned to see a huge hound running straight toward him, his natural reaction was to drop the ladder and take off. The ladder had a rope attached to it for tying it securely to whatever it was being set against. This was a bonus, as far as Coy was concerned. It would make moving the ladder to the front of the castle much easier.

The kitten tossed the rope over the dog's broad shoulders and chest. Exiting the building as quickly as possible, Huxley and Coy began moving the ladder around the front.

"Now Huxley, all we need is some paint," said the kitten to the hound laughing.

~

Inside the great hall, the party was slamming. It was packed from wall to wall, and the music was outstanding. The cats and other guests were eating and drinking, talking, and laughing at jokes. They were singing, dancing, and having a fantastic time all around.

Caterwaul sat on a fluffy pillow of red silk. He was enjoying himself more than words could say. Though it was never something he went looking for, he was definitely enjoying all of the attention. Muse sat on a matching cushion next to him. She was smiling too, delighted.

One by one, or sometimes in pairs, the guests all came forward to offer their respects. None wanted to be left out. It had been many years since the castle had seen an event like this. Every guest in attendance would take with them the hope of the future when they left that night.

Suddenly the music stopped, and the room went silent.

Caterwaul heard his name and snapped to attention. From the stage, Frankie the crooner was calling for him. As Caterwaul approached the stage, the crowd parted to make room. Frankie looked classy tonight, even more so than usual. His white fur was groomed perfectly, with the hair on his head combed back slick to show off his eyes. He wore a black tuxedo bow tie around his neck.

"This next song is dedicated to the cat who made all of this possible tonight. Some of you may not know him yet, but everyone here knows what he represents and what he means to this land and the folks living in it. If it wasn't for him, I wouldn't be here with you all tonight. He saved my life.

"So I'm singing this tune for my friend . . . for my companion, for my brother in arms . . . Let's have a round of applause for the lord of the castle, Sir Caterwaul . . . Who loves you, kitty?" He started clapping, and the room started to shake from all of the applause. "This song's called 'I've Got a Ball Made of String.'"

~

Tiny wanted to make a good impression on his boss. It was his first day on the job, but he was determined to prove his worth. Only a few days before, he was working as a grunt for the Felino family, and now he was employed as security at the castle. Talk about your twists of fate. He felt he had to do something big to make people put aside his past.

Still there was no action anywhere near his position. He had been stationed on the third floor of the castle, an area designated off-limits to the partygoers below. Suddenly he heard a loud noise. Running to the window, he saw a ladder being raised and set against the castle wall below him.

In the shadows, he caught sight of a very young cat running along a ledge above the main entrance. The ledge was only about fifteen feet below the window where he now stood. Tiny figured the little cat was up to no good. He could hear the youngster whispering to a co-conspirator on the ground below. If he had heard right, it had something to do with paint.

Minutes later a bucketful of paint and a brush were hoisted up to where the kitten waited. The little fellow set the container safely on the ledge and began moving it along. Tiny watched as he brought his brush up and down repeatedly dragging it against the outer wall of the castle.

He crept out of the window and hanging by his forepaws, dropped to the ledge below. The kitten was so busy laughing at his handiwork that he didn't notice the much larger cat coming near. On the ground, a dog started barking furiously.

"Got you, you little punk." Tiny shouted as he grabbed at the smaller cat's collar. Suddenly they began to fall. Reaching out to stop his descent, the former Felino pulled the paint bucket over with them. They hit the ground with a series of thuds.

Moments later, the doors of the great hall swung open. Standing in the doorway, roaring hysterically were Juan and Feliz. Between them, almost completely covered in blue paint, was a dog. Clutched in his mouth, he carried one of the new security recruits, who clutched in his hand a most embarrassed Coy. Like the dog, they were almost entirely blue.

At the sight of this disruption, the band stopped playing and laughter engulfed the hall.

"Your lordship," said Tiny the security cat, "I caught this kitten up on the roof changing the sign over the door. He was defacing your castle with this paint."

Caterwaul himself was roaring. Even covered as he was in a coat of thick paint, Caterwaul certainly recognized his friend Coy.

"Thank you for your attention to detail, my new friend. Let's see what these mischief-makers were up to, shall we?"

Caterwaul could barely get the words out, he was laughing so hard.

As Caterwaul and a crowd of his guests moved outside to see what had been done, Juan tapped Huxley on the hind leg to let him know to let go. The dog released Tiny, and Tiny let go of the blue kitten's collar.

Looking up to the space above the door, Caterwaul could see the lettering above the entrance was changed. The letters "hoon" had been covered up with paint so that the sign over the door now read Cat Castle.

"We wanted to surprise you," said Coy.

~

"Oh my word, what a kettle of fish this is. Whoever, even if he lived a hundred million years, coulda seen this coming? The once proud and great Queen Druciah, ruler of all she surveyed, reduced to this . . . a cat . . . and one with no tail no less."

These were the words of Edsel the Rat, without a doubt the most annoying animal in all of existence. He was beside himself, because now, the evil queen who had made his life a living hell was trapped inside the body of a cat. And to make matters worse, or better, depending on your perspective, it was the body of a cat with no tail.

"Hey Druciah, I got a joke for you. What did the queen say to her tail as it was being chopped off like?" He came running over to where she sat, trying to ignore him. He was careful to stay just out of her reach, however. "She said . . . Manx for the memories." He started laughing uproariously. "Ya get it? Cause a Manx is a cat that's got no tail."

Edsel liked to gloat. Never in his entire rodent existence did he have such an opportunity to gloat as this, to tear into a new addition to the Witch's family with abandon. He couldn't get enough. Druciah was about to get a kicking from a shoe which now was firmly on the other foot.

The Witch sat at her small dusty table, pondering her next move. *It is good to be able to have a real game again,* she thought. She slid her right hand knight up two and then one space to the right. Edsel the Rat sat on the arm of the chair beside her. He was ranting and raving as usual, pointing at the tailless white cat opposite the Witch. Neither the Witch nor her feline opponent paid him much attention.

The Witch was confident that she could either take her opponent's knight, or if she was really lucky, her left hand bishop. At that moment, a white paw came forward and took the Witch's knight with hers.

"That's your problem, Witch," said the white cat. "Always trying to see the game two and three moves out, sometimes you forget to protect yourself in the here and now."

The Witch smiled at her from across the table. She was happy to finally have some competition again. She'd missed this for so long. "The game is far from over, my friend. How do you know that I didn't just draw you into making that last move?" She cackled with delight, as Druciah suddenly got extra serious about analyzing her opponent's play.

Yes, it is good to have a friend again, thought the Witch of Red Moon Forest. She looked across at the cat as she imagined her next move.

"Well, Druciah," said the Witch jokingly. "At least you got your beauty back." She grinned at her opponent, "That's one in the plus column certainly. We will have to do something about your color, though."

CPSIA information can be obtained at www.ICGtesting.com
Printed in the USA
LVOW011051071111

253818LV00002B/1/P